c/o ARNOLD'S CORNERS

c/o ARNOLD'S CORNERS

by Suzanne Newton

THE WESTMINSTER PRESS
PHILADELPHIA

PUBLISHED BY THE WESTMINSTER PRESS ®
PHILADELPHIA, PENNSYLVANIA

PRINTED IN THE UNITED STATES OF AMERICA

Library of Congress Cataloging in Publication Data

Newton, Suzanne.
    C/o Arnold's Corners.

    SUMMARY: A twelve-year-old girl upsets her family and her small southern community when she befriends a "hippie" stranger, a young mother, and a black classmate.
    [1. Prejudices—Fiction]   I. Title.
PZ7.N4875Cab   [Fic]   73–18063
ISBN 0–664–32545–9

For Carl, who has always let me BE

Special acknowledgment to Calvin L. Criner, who thought of a title when the author could not, and to E. Stephen Edwards, M.D., for his help with the medical facts.

1

❀❀❀❀❀❀❀❀❀❀❀

A VW camper roared off the highway in a cloud of summer dust and bounced its way across rocks and gravel until it came to a stop in front of our store. The driver scrunched his head down and peered out of the window at me.

"Hey, young lady! Can anyone around here fill up this tank for me?"

"Yes, sir," I said in my best cool business voice. "May I have your tank key, please?"

He grinned. His teeth were white under a kind of short, handlebar mustache. His hair was very black and straight—and on the long side. He looked as though he might be part Indian. Except for the darkness of his coloring his face was sort of like the picture of Robert Louis Stevenson on the Author cards. I couldn't tell about his age, except that he was older than me and younger than Daddy.

"Women certainly are moving in," he said as I filled

the tank and wiped the windshield. "Taking jobs away from us men."

"No reason a girl can't fill a tank as well as a boy," I said and handed back the tank key. "That'll be two seventy-three."

He fished in his back pocket. The day was scorching, but he had on a long-sleeved purple shirt and rust-colored, close-fitting pants. It made me hot to look at him. I decided that where he came from must be either air-conditioned or a lot cooler than Arnold's Corners. Also a lot different. Men's fashions in Arnold's Corners run to overalls or Levi's.

The man pulled a credit card out of his wallet and handed it to me.

"Sorry," I told him. "We don't take credit cards here. Strictly cash."

He gave an exasperated sigh and took three one-dollar bills from the wallet. "I was counting on these three dollars buying my lunch and supper."

"I haven't been able to persuade Daddy to take credit cards," I apologized. "He doesn't believe in credit in any form."

He looked thoughtful. "May I use your phone to make a call?"

"We don't have one," I said. It was getting to be embarrassing. "Daddy says a telephone is a nuisance. It only rings when nobody's close enough to answer it. We don't even have one at home."

The man followed me into the store. I rang up the money and gave him his change. He looked at it and then glanced around, sniffing the air. I did not think that was strange. Our store smells musty like the livestock feed in the back room, and sweet like melted ice cream, and bitter like patent medicine, with a little bit of road dust and plug chewing tobacco mixed in to tickle the nose.

"Do you have something for twenty-seven cents that'll hold body and soul together until tomorrow?" he asked.

"How far are you going?" I stalled, thinking he might starve before he could get there.

"Nowhere. My camper and I have permission to park in some woods that belong to Mr. Lyman Hayes. Know him?"

I nodded. To my relief Daddy suddenly appeared at the doorway of the stock room, stamping the morning dew and dirt from his heavy boots. He looked the man over, and I could tell right away what he thought of the long hair and mustache, not to mention the purple shirt.

"Daddy, this is Mr.—uh—"

"King," the man said quickly. "Raoul King."

"Tal Brigham," said Daddy, holding out his hand.

"Mr. King's staying on Mr. Lyman Hayes's property for a while," I explained. "He needs some food, but he had to spend all his available cash on gas because Brigham's Store doesn't take credit cards."

"You ought to always ask," Daddy said, but I could tell that he was embarrassed.

"I expect a check in the mail tomorrow," said Mr. King. "I don't suppose you'd give me some food on credit until then?"

Daddy's face was stern. Mr. King answered his own question. "No, I guess not. Well, thanks anyway."

He started out of the store. I caught Daddy's eye, and although I didn't say anything, I thought very hard. Daddy blinked and turned a little red.

"Uh—wait just a minute, Mr. King!" He waved a

hand toward the shelves. "Pick up whatever you need between now and tomorrow. Rosalee here will keep account for you."

I let out my breath slowly.

"I appreciate that very much," Mr. King said, coming back to the counter.

Daddy looked as though he wished he had kept his mouth shut, but it was too late for that. Just then somebody came in for hog feed, and Daddy went to the back room with him. Mr. King walked around the store picking up things and bringing them to the counter.

I knew he probably didn't realize that to people in Arnold's Corners the fact that he was staying on Mr. Hayes's land was no recommendation. People here don't have much to do with Lyman Hayes for two reasons—he minds his own business and he keeps his mouth shut. For that he is called a hermit, and worse things too. I admire Mr. Hayes.

"This ought to do it," Mr. King said finally, putting a box of aspirin and a carton of Pepsis with the other things. I got out the sales pad and listed items and prices. They came to $7.24.

"You have pretty hair," he said suddenly.

I have not been so flabbergasted since James Lucas put a smushed frog on my desk last year.

Mr. King laughed. "Hasn't anyone ever told you that you have pretty hair?"

I shook my head and wondered how anybody could think two red pigtails were pretty.

"It's the color," he said. "The auburn with copper highlights—and the dark-brown eyes."

I did not know what to say. I have been called "Red" all my life, and I guess I have always thought of myself like that. I snapped open a big paper sack and put his stuff inside very fast. I gave him the carbon copy of his list. I was putting our copy in the cash register drawer when Daddy returned from the stock room.

"I hope you got what you needed," he said. He did not sound too friendly.

"Yes, thanks. See you tomorrow—with cash," Mr. King replied, touching a hand to his forehead.

When he was gone, Daddy came over to the cash register. "How much?"

"Seven twenty-four," I replied. Daddy looked thoughtful. "Wonder how come a long-haired fellow like that would be getting money in the mail?"

I shrugged. Probably Mr. King would be the cause of a lot of wondering in Arnold's Corners.

Daddy looked up at the Coca-Cola clock on the wall. "You'd better go back to the house, Rosalee. Your mother might need you to help with the baby."

I made a face. "What if somebody comes in the store while you're in back? They could steal you blind and you'd never know."

"I managed this store for four years before you were ever born, and I have done a fairly good job of managing it since," he answered, pretending to be insulted. "Nobody has ever robbed me yet—except for a small, Chiclet-snitching redhead who hangs around here!"

Daddy is almost as big a tease as the men who come to the store. He knows he couldn't do without my help. At least my services are cheap and I work hard. However, I do not like to be taken for granted, even by my own kin. "How would you like it if I went to work for Mr. Hooker?" I asked, to test him.

Daddy snorted. "The question is, How would *Hooker* like it?"

Mr. Hooker's store is down the highway from ours,

just across from the Lacy Creek School. He and Daddy are rivals. Both stores sell pretty much the same kind of stuff, but Daddy gets the jump on Mr. Hooker by selling seed, feed, and fertilizer. Bent City is just far enough away to make going there for farm supplies a nuisance, so Daddy does a steady year-round business, although the summers are slacker for feed and fertilizer than the rest of the year.

The main thing that makes them rivals, though, is the post office. For years when the Democrats were in, Daddy was Arnold's Corners' acting postmaster. When the Republicans were in, Mr. Hooker got the job. During my lifetime Daddy has had more opportunity to serve than Mr. Hooker. They have to take a Civil Service examination. The last time, they both made the same score on the exam, so Mr. Hooker, being of the acceptable party, got another chance. All the equipment and stuff had to be moved out of our store and down the highway to Mr. Hooker's. It left an empty partitioned corner up front near the door. I begged Daddy to fill it with some kind of display, but he said no, Hooker wasn't going to be postmaster all that long, and he didn't want to go to the trouble of moving everything for such a little while. Daddy has his stubborn streak.

"Mr. Hooker might like it fine, to have a trained expert like me," I said. "I may go to his store this very afternoon and ask him."

"You do that," said Daddy, "and don't forget who trained you. Now—go home, and don't forget to take along those books you got from the County Bookmobile this morning."

He needn't have worried. I would never forget my books! I can only get ten at a time when the Bookmo-

12

bile comes to our store each month. I always tell myself that I'll read them slowly, so they will last, but it is hard to live up to the resolution.

I held five books in each arm and crossed the highway quickly to keep my feet from blistering on the hot asphalt.

The road to our house is not paved—in fact, nothing is paved in Arnold's Corners except the highway running through. Arnold's Corners isn't a town. It's more of a community. I think it may have started to be a town years and years ago, when trains were the main transportation, but now the trains don't run anymore.

Daddy calls our road "Widows Row," because most of the people who live along there are old ladies with dead husbands and grown children. Except for Ruthie Chapman, Timmy and I are about the only kids, and Timmy's just a baby, like Ruthie. Everybody told me that having a brother or sister was pretty special, but I want you to know there is nothing so special about a squalling, time-consuming baby. I am now a one-hundred-percent expert on diaper-changing, bottle feeding, prune-spitting, and baby-toting. He certainly worked a slowdown in our family life. For the past year Mom has been tired a lot. Now that he is at the wigglesome stage, one of us always has to stay home with Timmy, or else take him along on our trips, which is worse than staying home with him, if you ask me. That is why I have spent as much time as possible at the store since school let out for the summer. Mom doesn't like that. She says a young lady has no business hanging around a store full of men.

Arnold's Corners doesn't boast any factories or famous people, but I've no doubt it would win hands down in a contest for Gossip Capital of the World. Of course, we have our mysteries the same as anywhere, but folks here can hardly bear a mystery. They feel compelled to get to the bottom of everything, whether it is any of their business or not. It usually isn't.

Jenny Chapman is one of our mysteries. I admire her tremendously. She has lived in Arnold's Corners for months and nobody knows any more about her than they did when she came. She can really keep her mouth shut! Jenny showed up one day with the baby—that's Ruthie—and a U-Haul truck. Folks around here nearly went crazy trying to guess who she was and why she was in Arnold's Corners! But there was nobody to find out from except Jenny. She is not telling.

She rented the old tumbledown house where Mr. Lehigh used to store some of his cured tobacco and put out a wooden sign that said SEWING AND ALTERING. She has been swamped with work ever since. Ladies went at first hoping she'd slip up and tell something on herself, but so far as I know she has not. Now they go because she can sew better than any of them. Some people do not care for her because she does not confide the secrets of her life. *I* think she is brave—it is lonesome not to have someone to talk to.

Jenny and I got acquainted soon after she came. I was trying to talk Mrs. Chips, the Bookmobile lady, into letting me have more than ten books. The argument was not going well for me, because she has to serve the whole county with that little handful of a library.

Jenny was so quiet I did not know she had come in until she spoke.

"Could each of us get ten books and then trade during the month?"

It was the first time I had seen her up close, although

of course I knew who she was. I liked the way she smiled all the way up to her eyes. She carried her baby in a papoose-looking thing on her back. I must confess I stared, as I had never seen a baby carried like that in real life.

Mrs. Chips looked her up and down. "Surely—if you want to."

I was mystified. "Do you really want to do that?" I said. "I don't read very grown-up books—"

Jenny just smiled. "I'll take a chance."

I finally remembered my manners. "I'm Rosalee Brigham. My daddy owns the store."

"Yes. I've seen you ride by on your bicycle."

That was all. We did not ask each other any questions because we were both satisfied with what we saw. Mrs. Chips helped her fill out a card—using my daddy as a reference unbeknownst to him—and we became book-trading friends. As a result, I have had a chance to read *To Kill a Mockingbird, The Catcher in the Rye, Gone with the Wind,* and others that are much more interesting than Nancy Drew mysteries and such kid stuff.

Now I was close enough to her house to see her sitting on the front porch rocker with a lapful of material, her needle going in and out. Ruthie sat on a quilt beside her, playing with the spools of thread in the sewing basket. I shifted the books and walked faster.

It is a pleasure to see what Jenny has done to the old house. Until she came nobody had lived in it for fifteen years, and it was a mess. She cleaned it up and planted petunias along the front path and beside the porch. She made bright curtains for the old bay window. Mr. Lehigh has never painted the outside of the house, but it doesn't matter—the place has sparkle all the same.

When I am old and have finished my world travels, I
shall buy an ancient house and make something of it,
the way Jenny has done.

"Hey!" I yelled, when I was almost upon them.

Jenny looked up and smiled. Ruthie waved both
hands, lost her balance, and began rolling down the
sloping porch.

"Watch it!" I yelled, dropping the books. I took one
huge leap, trying to catch Ruthie, tripped over the
SEWING AND ALTERING sign, and sprawled across the petunias.

2

❀❀❀❀❀❀❀❀❀❀❀❀

Thump!

The baby landed in the middle of my back and rolled over onto the ground. Then she began to howl. I lay still, trying to get my breath while petunias tickled my nose. Jenny clattered down the steps. Spools and pins rolled off the porch and dropped to the right and left of me.

"Rosalee! Are you all right?"

I raised up on one elbow and nodded my head. "Yeah. Is Ruthie hurt?"

Ruthie was fine. As soon as I spoke she stopped crying and stared at me. I had to laugh, even though I felt like one big bruise.

"Oh, you!" Jenny scolded Ruthie, picking her up and dusting her off. She sounded as exasperated as Mom does sometimes. But it is a lot of wasted breath to get mad at babies.

"You saved her life," Jenny said.

"That's not so," I said, getting to my feet. "If I hadn't

17

yelled out like that, she wouldn't have lost her balance in the first place."

"It would have happened sooner or later," Jenny sighed, pushing back her long hair with one impatient hand. "She's into everything. I don't dare do any sewing while she's awake unless she's in the playpen. She needs a . . . a keeper! Look—everything's scattered—"

"I'll hold her while you look for the stuff that fell off the porch," I offered.

A few minutes later Jenny climbed the steps and put the things into the sewing basket. "I haven't found it all, but I'll look again when she's asleep."

I suddenly remembered the books I had dropped at the edge of the yard.

"I got new books," I said, shifting Ruthie to one hip. "I didn't see you at the Bookmobile this morning. I was busy inside the store. What did you get this time?"

Jenny shook her head and began folding the material that lay on the porch rocker. "I didn't."

"Didn't get any books?"

"Sorry!" she said sharply. "I don't have time to read anymore."

"Gosh—I'm sorry," I said.

Jenny held out her hands for Ruthie. I was relieved to hand her over—she is extremely wigglesome. Jenny hugged her close for a moment, but she was not thinking about Ruthie. She looked tired and hopeless, and I was sorry—but I did not know what I could do about it.

"I have to be going," I said. Jenny nodded. Ruthie waved one fat hand and babbled something nobody but another baby could understand. I looked back once, when I was on the road again, but they had gone inside.

After the hot, dusty walk, the wide shade of the two oak trees in our yard was a welcome sight. And luck was with me—Timmy wasn't in the playpen in the living room.

My room used to be the den. It is right next to the living room. I managed to slip in without being seen and had time to read five chapters before lunch. That is about the only advantage of having a bedroom in such a public place. I used to have the other room upstairs, but Mom wanted Timmy to be close by if he cried during the night, so I was moved.

Randy Mitchell sometimes goes to the store at noon to stay so Daddy can come home. When I came into the kitchen, Daddy was already at the table. I pulled out my chair and sat down.

"Something has to be done about you," Mom said without preliminary. "You hang around the store, and when you come home, you immediately stick your nose in a book. Why, I didn't even know you had come home until your daddy told me! Why don't you go out and make friends?"

I have tried to explain to Mom that a person doesn't want to be with just anybody. You want a friend you can trust to keep your secrets and respect your way of doing things. I have learned that from bitter experience.

"I've been thinking I might get a job," I said, changing the subject.

"A job?" Mom exclaimed.

"What has gotten into you?" Daddy wanted to know. "What do you need another job for? Don't you earn enough money working for me?"

"I'd like to earn some money that doesn't come out of your pocket," I said. I thought that reason would appeal to him more than the real one, which was this—I had to stay away from the house so as not to read all of my books at once. Without Jenny's ten, it was going to be a lean month!

"Girls going on thirteen aren't in great demand on the labor market these days," said Daddy. "Where are you thinking of applying?"

"I thought you'd remember our conversation this morning," I said. "At Hooker's Store, of course." The answer surprised me as much as it did them.

"You can't be serious, Rosalee!" Mom gasped.

"I know how it must look to you," I said, "if you are thinking in terms of family loyalty. But look at it from a more practical angle. I could spy out the merchandise and let Daddy know what Mr. Hooker is going to charge for one thing and another."

Daddy almost choked. "*I* don't care what Hooker charges—it isn't going to make any difference in *my* prices!"

"Rosalee has lost her mind," Mom said to the ceiling.

"On second thought, Elizabeth," Daddy said, "she might have something." The lines around his eyes crinkled, as though he might burst out laughing any minute. He looked at me over the rim of his iced tea glass. "I hear Hooker's pretty tight with his money. You might not make much for the amount of work you do. I'll bet he'd charge you ten cents for an ice-cream sandwich, too, instead of letting you have it for a nickel the way I've been doing."

"True," I said, "but then maybe I need the discipline of having to pay the retail price for everything. All your other customers do."

Daddy was caught and he knew it, but he took his time chewing the next mouthful.

"Tal Brigham, I hope you—" Mom began.

"I don't see what harm it'll do for her to ask for a job, Elizabeth," Daddy said. "I doubt she'll get it, anyhow."

He left soon afterward to go back to the store.

"I'll straighten the kitchen and wash the dishes before I go see Mr. Hooker," I told Mom. "Why don't you go up and take a nap while Timmy's asleep?"

She gave me such a grateful look I was ashamed for not offering before. I guess I always had the idea I would not do things to suit her. She went right upstairs. By the time I finished wiping the table, sweeping the kitchen floor, and washing dishes, I had had a stomach full of housework for one day. I don't see how Mom can go at it with such dedication. It bores me to death.

Mr. Hooker couldn't help knowing how well qualified I was to work in his store. I did not see how he could refuse this opportunity to hire experienced labor cheap. I did not intend to ask for a big salary—maybe only fifty cents an hour. That would be four dollars for an eight-hour day, twenty dollars a week, which isn't bad for a person my age. It sounded so good I had to remind myself that I wasn't doing it for the money.

The sun is fierce at 2 P.M. in June in Arnold's Corners. That is one of the dubious joys of living in the southeastern United States. To keep from having a heat stroke I wore my straw sombrero with the little bingle balls around the brim. My aunt brought it from Mexico. The front yard wasn't so shady anymore. I was squinting into the sun and had reached the gate before I noticed a pony and rider coming along the road. They were heading toward the highway—little gray Baby Doll with May Thomas on her back. May was riding without a saddle, and her long mahogany legs hung down so far her feet almost touched the ground. We are the same age and have both lived in Arnold's Corners all our lives, but we did not know each other until a year ago when the Negro and white schools were consolidated. It seems funny in such a little place for people to live side by side for years and hardly know one another, but that is how it was. Her daddy farms for Bonnie Lewis' father, who is a man of considerable means and property—a fact that Bonnie will not let anybody overlook.

I was about to call to May when I caught sight of Bonnie herself, riding Hobie, her pinto, a good twenty yards behind May. She kept pulling on Hobie's reins to keep him at a walk, as though to make sure she would not catch up with May. I almost turned around and went back into the house. If it hadn't been for May, I would have.

May's smile is about as broad and cheerful as anything you will ever see. I like her because she doesn't let trifles bother her, and that is a real gift.

"Hey!" she called. "You going up the road? I'll give you a ride!"

"We'll break Baby Doll's back, the two of us," I said, but I went out to meet her just the same.

"Naw—you're little for your age," May said. She has a husky, deep voice. It makes a person sit up and take notice. If I had a voice like that to go with my cool business face, I could go places.

I jerked my head in the direction of the straggler. "What about your friend back there? She seems to be having trouble catching up."

May hooted. "We started out together from Mr. Lewis' tobacco shed, but time we got to the road she was finding reasons to hang back. We finished work early today so we figured we'd come up to your daddy's store for something to cool off. Gollee, it's hot!"

I climbed up behind her. May is lean and her hair is cropped short. When she reaches her full height she is going to be about six feet tall. She will be a commanding figure.

We plodded along, not saying much. Some people you have to talk to. Some are just comfortable to be with. I have hardly seen May since school was out—we don't go to the same church or anything, but when we do get together it's the same as if we saw each other every day.

We heard trotting hooves behind us and we both turned to look at the same time. Bonnie had managed to cover that twenty-yard gap. She must have thought we would talk about her if she didn't hurry and catch up. I don't know why—she knows I don't gossip. Her round face was bright pink from too much sun. The freckles stood out like pennies on a plate. Hobie lunked along with his head down as though he wished he were a hundred miles away in a cool, green pasture. I couldn't blame him. I have some idea of what it is like to have Bonnie Lewis on your back, though not in a literal sense. It is hard for me to believe now that she and I used to be best friends.

"Y'all go too fast for me!" she said in a sweet, honey-pie voice.

May didn't say anything.

"You going to the store, Rosalee?" Bonnie went on.

"To Hooker's," I said, before I thought.

Bonnie was suddenly all ears and gleaming eyes. "Why in the world are you going to Hooker's?"

"For the mail, of course," I fibbed.

"I guess you wish the P.O. was still at Brigham's," Bonnie said, pushing back her blond curls. "It must be embarrassing, having to go to Mr. Hooker to ask for stamps and all."

Bonnie is going to grow up to be like a lot of other ladies in Arnold's Corners.

"Oh, I don't know," I said, swaying my body with Baby Doll's pony waddle. "All that equipment took up a lot of room at the store."

I found out last year that Bonnie and I have different ideas about forgivable and unforgivable. The same school bus picks up all of us. May's littlest brother, Ed, was in first grade and so shy he would not talk to anybody. James Lucas started out the year picking on him —making him get up from his seat on the bus and things like that. It made May and her older brother, Bud, furious, but they wouldn't fight about it. I guess their folks had made them promise not to. So one of them would hold Ed or give him their seat. I got so mad at James I could hardly stand him, but when I told him so, he just laughed.

Then one day while our class was out for recess and the first-graders were lined up to go into the building, James stuck out a foot and tripped Ed on the steps so he cut his chin. I saw it plain as anything. I told our teacher, but since she didn't see it happen she would not do anything about it.

So I followed James around the playground until he was close to the muddy drainage ditch that runs between the school grounds and the highway. I waited until his back was turned, and then I ran with my hands straight out in front of me and pushed him flat in the ditch! He did not know what hit him until I hol-

lered to him down in the mud, "You'd better quit picking on little guys or you will get worse than that!"

He came up out of the ditch sputtering and swinging
his arms like a crazy windmill. I didn't budge. He
looked so silly I was not even scared of him.

"Don't you lay a hand on me," I said between my
teeth, "and don't you bother Ed anymore either. If you
do, I will tell Mr. Paley who pulled up the school mailbox and put it in the boys' bathroom last week, and he
will have no trouble believing me at all!"

James turned four shades of red, one after the other.
Then he said a bad word and walked off. He has not
had much of a complimentary nature to say to me
since, but I do not care. He has not bothered Ed anymore.

Bonnie came up beside me as soon as James walked
away. "Why did you have to go treat James like that
over a little colored boy! James was just teasing. Gosh,
you're so *dumb* when it comes to boys!"

Well, maybe that is so, but I am not like Bonnie in
that respect. She likes for boys to notice that she is a
girl, and I do not. Besides, it made me mad that she
didn't care what James did to Ed. Our relationship
cooled considerably from that day.

We passed Jenny's house. Since there are no trees in
the front yard, the sun bakes her porch. No doubt it
was hot in her living room, but through the bay window we could see her bent over her work at the sewing
machine.

"I wouldn't live in a place like that!" Bonnie said.

"It's about as good as where *we* live," May said
matter-of-factly. That was a jab, as Bonnie's daddy
owns the house where the Thomases live and it is a

25

well-known fact that he does not offer his tenants the best living quarters in the world. However, the remark was lost on Bonnie.

"You'd live there if you couldn't afford better," I said.

"I'd get married, that's what I'd do," Bonnie said with a toss of her head. "With her good looks, why doesn't she get married? My mother says that at least three different men have proposed to Jenny Chapman and she's turned them all down. Mother says she bets Jenny's never even *had* a husband!"

I did not ask how Bonnie's mother happened to have so much information. Jenny doesn't tell anybody anything—I know that. No doubt the whole story had been made up by some woman whose creative juices work overtime.

"I'll get off here," I said as we neared the highway. "Thanks a lot."

"If you come over some morning, I'll let you ride all you want to," May said as I got down.

"Does your daddy know you're going to Hooker's?" Bonnie shouted over her shoulder. She had already crossed the highway and left May behind. I did not waste my breath answering her. I patted Baby Doll on the nose and gave her a stale oatmeal cookie I'd been keeping in the pocket of my shorts. She's a sweet pony. I wish she were mine.

3

✿✿✿✿✿✿✿✿✿✿✿

Except for some wasps buzzing near the gasoline pumps, there was no sign of life around Hooker's Store —no customers, no cars, not even a stray dog. I was strongly tempted to walk right on by, but I knew I had to go in, mostly because I had bragged to Daddy. Someday I will learn to keep my mouth shut. I took a deep breath and put on my cool business face.

Hooker's Store used to be a house. It has a porch roof that sticks out over the front, but no porch under it— just gravel and dirt. You have to go up little rickety wooden steps to get inside. There's no screen on the door. Inside it is so dim and narrow you feel as though you've walked into a boxcar. I haven't been inside many times.

When my eyes got used to the dimness, I was heart-ened to see that Hooker could certainly use some help. The candy bin had so many greasy fingerprints it was hard to tell what kind of candy he was selling. The floor was littered with cigarette butts and smushed candy wrappers. Flies were everywhere. Frankly, it turned my stomach, but I tried not to show it. That is no way to get a job, insulting people. My daddy runs a clean store. He sweeps out twice a day—or at least I do—and has screens on the doors and windows.

I didn't see anybody in the store. Much relieved, I said under my breath, "Well, that's that!" and started out the door.

Mr. Hooker's voice snatched out at me from somewhere. "Well, well! Little Red Brigham! What can I do for you?"

It startled me so the hair on the back of my neck prickled.

"I'm in the post office," he said. "Your daddy already got the mail."

"Yes, sir, I know that." I walked over to the post office window and peered in. He was sitting in one corner, writing. I recognized all the little stamping things we used to have when the post office was in our store. It even smelled somewhat the same. It made me kind of homesick. I leaned closer for a better sniff.

Mr. Hooker stopped writing and got up. I don't think he liked me to lean on his post-office counter like that. He is a round, short, little man with thick lips and very pink cheeks. He always wears green-striped shirts.

"I suppose you want to buy a stamp," he said, yanking open the drawer.

"Yes—no. I mean, I'd like to, but I didn't bring enough money."

"They only cost a few cents apiece!"

"I know. But I haven't written the letter yet. To tell the truth," I said in a hurry, before I lost my nerve, "I didn't come for a stamp at all. I came . . . to see if you might have a job for me."

When Mr. Hooker is astounded his eyes get very round and glassy-looking. It makes him resemble a goldfish.

"Did you say—a job?"

"Yes, sir. I've learned a lot from Daddy about working in stores and I thought . . ."

All of a sudden I wondered what I did think. The idea was not quite so remarkable as it had seemed earlier in the day. I looked out from under my sombrero. For some reason my knees were trembling. It was very embarrassing.

"A job, huh."

"I'm good at sweeping, dusting, and picking up," I said. "You know I've worked for Daddy for years."

"I bet he don't pay you," said Mr. Hooker.

"He does too!"

"Has he ever told you about child labor?"

I had to admit the term was new to me.

"There is a law that forbids a commercial enterprise to hire a youngster your age. Even at sixteen you're only allowed to work a certain number of hours a week. Maybe your daddy can get around it, but I couldn't."

"Are you trying to tell me my daddy is breaking the law?"

"I'm just telling you that if I put you on my payroll, *I'd* be breaking the law!"

I was sorry I had come. I tried to act cool as I backed toward the door. "I can certainly see your position," I said. "I wouldn't want you to get in trouble because of me. Good-by, Mr. Hooker."

"Good-by, Little Red. Feel free to drop in anytime— for a stamp or something."

He was laughing at me. I despise to be laughed at. I

backed right out the door—and into someone broad as a wall and twice as tall as I was.

"Whoa!" the man shouted as we both began to topple. My sombrero tipped forward over my eyes as I grabbed for the side of the door, and the man stumbled backward down the rickety steps.

"Gosh, I'm sorry!" I panted, yanking the sombrero from over my face. "I wasn't watch—"

It was Mr. Raoul King. He had changed into T-shirt, Bermudas, and sandals in honor of Arnold's Corners' climate, but the mustache-covered smile and the long hair were the same, even though he was sitting on the gravel at the bottom of the steps in a rather undignified manner.

"Oh, gosh!" I said again. It was not my day.

"Buenos días, Señorita Brigham," he said, taking note of my Mexican headgear. "What a pleasure to see you again!"

"I'll bet," I said, hurrying down the steps. "I am sorry! I should have been watching." I stood there wondering whether I ought to help him up. "Are you all right?"

Mr. King sprang to his feet and dusted off his Bermudas. "Perfectly." He did not seem at all annoyed. "Do you do business with your father's rival?"

That was an unexpected question—Mr. King certainly caught on fast for having been in Arnold's Corners such a short time. I turned to see if Mr. Hooker might be listening, then shook my head. "N-no. I was here on an errand of a—um—personal nature."

Unlike the typical Arnold's Corners citizen, Mr. King accepted that. He said, "I came to see whether my check might have arrived in the afternoon mail. I can

30

bring your father his seven twenty-four if it has. I don't like to owe money."

"The only mail delivery is early in the morning," I told him.

"Oh, well. No need to bother then. Could I take you somewhere?"

The temptation was very strong—I have always longed to ride in a camper. All the same, I knew what Mom and Daddy would think if I accepted the offer of a ride from a virtual stranger.

"I'm only going to our store," I said, while I made up my mind. "You'd hardly get started."

"No matter. I'd be honored," said Mr. King. "Of the people I have met in Arnold's Corners, you are the one I like best."

What do you say when a person says a thing like that to you, especially if you just finished knocking him down some steps? I certainly did not know, so I let him open the camper door for me and I got in.

I tried not to stare too hard. The inside was much bigger than I had thought it would be. There was a little sink and a table, a folding bed, a stove, and some cabinets. Everything was shining clean.

"I'm like a turtle, carrying my house around with me this way," Mr. King said as he settled into the driver's seat. "It's very convenient."

I nodded. What fun it would be to live in one of these and to drive to a new place every day! Or to stay in one place as long as you liked, the way Mr. King was doing. I sneaked another look over my shoulder. Housekeeping wouldn't take any time at all in a camper like this. I decided that when I began my world travels I would go in a camper.

"A penny for your thoughts," said Mr. King as he started the motor and moved out to the highway.

I don't think a grown-up had ever wanted to hear what I thought. To my shame, I got kind of gushy. "I was thinking how great it would be to have this kind of house. Everybody should have one!"

"The highways would be crowded," he said. "Besides, this isn't for everybody. Most people like curtains and carpets and shiny kitchens. They wouldn't care for the nomadic life."

"I would," I told him. "I do not intend to live my life chasing dirt. There are too many exciting things to do."

"Oh?"

"Yes. I am going to travel from place to place and change my name everyday if I want to. And I'm not going to tell anyone anything about myself—they'll have to take me the way they see me!"

"You are certainly wise for one so young," he said. His smile was friendly, not teasing.

"Being young doesn't mean you have to be dumb," I told him.

"No, of course not," he chuckled. "Maybe you're at the smartest age of all."

"I have never met a grown-up who believed that," I said.

"Maybe you haven't met one who would admit to believing it. But you're at a time in life when you have the gift of double vision."

"The gift of double vision?" I frowned. "It sounds more like a handicap!"

"I suppose it could be," he said. "Depends upon your point of view. It can be painful, sure enough, but that's not always a bad thing. Anyway, I mean that you can look backward and understand how it is to be a child, and at the same time you can understand grown-ups almost better than they understand themselves."

I was astounded, not only by what he said, but by the fact that he said it to me. "Why is it like that?" I asked.

He raised his eyebrows. "I don't know—perhaps it's because you're in between—not a child, not an adult."

We were almost to the store and I was glad. I am not used to deep conversations with strangers. Baby Doll and Hobie were tethered on the shady side of the building. I crossed my fingers and hoped Bonnie would stay inside until Mr. King left.

"Thanks a lot for the ride," I said quickly as he pulled up in front of the store. I opened the door and jumped to the ground.

"Tell your father I'll be by again as soon as my ship comes in." And with a wave and a grin he was gone.

Bonnie stood gawking in the doorway. She got right to the point. "Who was that? Haven't your folks ever told you not to accept rides from strangers?" She said it plenty loud, so Daddy would be sure to hear.

"He is not a stranger," I said, marching past her into the store. Inside, May was licking the last of a chocolate popsicle while she read the poster of coming attractions at Bent City Theater. She winked, which made me take heart.

"His name is Mr. King," I went on. "He does business with us. Hello, Daddy!"

"Hello, yourself." He was opening a new case of rubbing alcohol. "Do you have a minute to put these on the shelf for me? I have to make out an order."

"Yes, sir," I said. I took off the sombrero, which was making my head sweat, and hung it on a nail by the headache-pill calendar. Out of the corner of my eye I saw that Bonnie wasn't wasting any time starting home.

May stayed a minute longer. "I meant that about coming to ride the pony," she said, darting a look at Daddy's back.

"O.K.," I said. "I'd like to."

A few moments after she went out I heard Baby Doll's hooves clop across the highway and thud on the dirt road.

"See you drove up with that Mr. King," Daddy said.

"Yes, sir. He was leaving Mr. Hooker's the same time I was." The alcohol bottles clinked together lightly as I lined them up like soldiers, one behind the other.

"Did you get the job?" Daddy asked.

I had almost forgotten about the job. It all came back in an embarrassing rush. "Nope. Why didn't you tell me about child labor?"

"About what?"

"Child labor. Mr. Hooker claims that a person under sixteen isn't supposed to work and that if he hired me, he'd be breaking the law."

"Well, maybe he couldn't put you on the payroll exactly, but—"

"Do you have me on the payroll?"

"Of course not! I pay you out of my pocket, just as when you do home chores. Hooker could do that, too, if he had a mind to. He's just too penny-pinching!"

I had never heard my daddy speak that way of Mr. Hooker. "He made it sound as though you had been breaking the law—said you were 'getting around it.'"

"Pshaw!" Daddy snorted. "He ought to be ashamed of himself, saying such a thing. The law says that I couldn't hire you to work a forty-hour week, but it's all right for you to do little picking-up jobs around the

34

store." He frowned furiously at the order book. "How'd you happen to take up with that Mr. King? Was he trading at Hooker's?"

I did not like the way he kept saying "that Mr. King." I explained how I had happened to run into Mr. King, except that I didn't mention that I had actually run into him.

"Did you find out what he is doing here?"

"No," I said. "I didn't see that it was any of my business to ask."

"You ought to be careful about getting in a car with somebody you don't know very well," Daddy said, closing the order book with a bang.

I looked at his face. It was blank. Of all the faces that grown-ups put on, that is the one I despise most. It means that whatever they are telling you is very important and critical to them, but they don't want you to ask why, so they try to keep their face and voice as usual. It never works. They are trying too hard.

"I am careful," I said.

Daddy put his hands in his pockets and went over to the window to look out at the highway.

"May Thomas invite you over to her house?" he asked, after a while.

"Yes."

"You thinking seriously of going?"

"I might."

"I don't know as you should do that," he said, pursing his lips. "One thing leads to another."

"Like what?"

The little muscles twitched in his cheeks and jaws. "You need to consider the looks of things," he said, making his voice reasonable. "How things are done in our community. It's fine for you to be nice to May—I'm glad you are. But visiting back and forth—that's another thing altogether."

"We go to the same school now," I said.

"Yes, but that's different."

I did not say anything. He gave an exasperated sigh and started toward the stock room. "I don't have anything for you to do here. Might as well go home. Get yourself a pushup out of the freezer before you go."

That surprised me—he doesn't usually invite me to get a pushup.

"Do I have to go home?"

"You didn't get the job, did you?"

"Well, I haven't exhausted all my resources," I said. "Mr. Hooker isn't the only person around here who needs experienced help!" I sounded a lot more sure of the fact than I felt. I opened the ice-cream cabinet and leaned way over to get the full benefit of the cool vapor in my face.

"You could work in tobacco, the way other kids do," Daddy suggested. "Bonnie says she's already earned right much and the season's barely started."

I made a face. He knows I despise to work in tobacco. It's good money all right, but you earn every penny. It is sticky work. Gum comes off the leaf and makes you itch, and then the flies and gnats swarm around and you can't swat without leaving a sticky smudge somewhere else on you. I don't think I am too *good* to work in tobacco. I just don't like it.

"You needn't turn up your nose at honest work," he said.

"For me, it wouldn't be honest work," I told him as I started out the door. "I would hate every minute of it— I'd only be doing it for the money, and that isn't honest if you don't *need* the money."

"What kind of a notion is that! What's the good of working, then?" he hollered after me.

"To keep away from the house so I won't read all my books at once," I said, but I didn't say it loud enough for him to hear. I walked out into the afternoon sunlight, so bright it made the top of my eyeballs ache. I cooled my tongue in the sherbet and wondered how many people in the world spent long, tiresome days doing honest work.

4

✿✿✿✿✿✿✿✿✿✿✿✿

Although the sun was still high and bright, it was the downward side of the afternoon. I thought about the ten unread books on my night table. After such a discouraging day I deserved to read one of them. I now recognized that there was considerable truth in Daddy's statement that girls my age weren't in great demand on the labor market, no matter how eager they might be for something to do.

Poor Jenny—*she* certainly didn't have to look around for something to do. I considered how uneven life was, to give some people more than their share of hard labor and others not enough. I remembered how discouraged she sounded that morning. Ruthie probably was tired of staying put—babies are like dogs and cats: they don't like to be penned in. I thought about little old wigglesome Timmy and wondered how Mom would manage if she did not have me around to watch him when she was doing the housework.

That's when the Big Idea hit me. I stopped dead in my tracks. Gosh, was I stupid not to have thought of it before!

I ran all the way to Jenny's house. This time I did not belly flop into the petunias. I jumped over the SEWING AND ALTERING sign, took the three steps in one leap, and hit the porch with a thud.

Jenny was at the door in an instant, looking scared to death. I keep forgetting that grown-ups have a tendency to misinterpret noise and yelling.

"What on earth has happened?" she said.

"Nothing—yet!" I panted. "Can I come in?"

"I think you'd better, before you explode." She held the door open, and I went ahead of her into the front room. The air was stifling. It was as if all the garments and materials piled on chairs and hanging from racks had absorbed and held every bit of heat that came through that bay window.

"Come to the kitchen," she said. "I'm cooking our supper now so Ruthie can go to bed early. It was too hot for her to sleep this afternoon."

I followed her through the middle room, which served as a bedroom. Ruthie was sitting in the playpen in the kitchen, but she pulled herself to her feet when we came in. She began to fret, just the way Timmy does when everybody but him is out moving around.

I had never been in Jenny's kitchen. Two small hamburgers sizzled in a frying pan on the kerosene stove. An iron sink stuck out from the wall. You could see all the pipes. Whoever put it there must have been a short person—even I would have to bend over to do dishes in it. Except for a small round table and two chairs and a little refrigerator the room was bare. There were no cabinets—just shelves over the sink. I thought of Mr. King's camper and wondered if Jenny would like it as much as I did.

"This is the very hardest time of day for Ruthie," Jenny was saying, "especially when she's so tired—and bored with the playpen. She has to stay in it so much—"

"Look—" I interrupted, hardly able to stand still. "I want you to do me a favor."

"All right," she said. She did not sound overjoyed. She motioned for me to sit down at the oilcloth-covered table. "If you want me to sew for you, it may be a while . . ."

I shook my head. "I want you to let me come and baby-sit for you for two hours every day, while you sew!" I could not keep the grin off my face, especially when her mouth dropped open and she looked at me as if she saw a saint in a burning bush or something. Her eyes lighted up, just for a second. Then they looked tired again. She shook her head.

"Sorry," she said, flipping the two hamburgers in a cloud of greasy steam. "I couldn't pay you what it's worth to me. On my budget ten cents an hour is the most I could afford, and that's ridiculous."

"You don't understand," I said, waving my arms around in the air. "The money doesn't matter. I'll do it for ten cents an hour—or even less. You'd be doing me a tremendous favor!" I told her about my unfortunate experience at Mr. Hooker's.

"You see," I wound up, "it'll work out for both of us. I'll have a job that will keep me away from home so I won't read all my books at once. You'll have more time to sew, so you can catch up, and you'll have time to read again, and then next month you can get ten books and I can get ten, and we'll both have time to read." I sat back in the chair, feeling somewhat pleased.

Jenny sat down in the other chair. For a moment she just sat there, and then she began to laugh. She laughed till the tears rolled down her cheeks. I did not see what was funny.

"Rosalee Brigham, no one else in all of Berry County could have come up with such an idea!"

"You mean it's O.K.?" I leaped to my feet and nearly knocked over the table.

"Sit down," she told me, getting serious. "Your mother has a baby, too—remember? She needs your help at home. And your father couldn't get alon without you at the store. You have to find out what they think of your idea, then come back tomorrow, and we'll talk about it again."

"I could let you know tonight," I said. "They know I'm looking for a job."

She shook her head. "Give them time to think about it. And you, too—you'd better think about it."

"I did—"

She held up her hand. "Probably your parents wouldn't mind if—if you baby-sat for someone else. But they might have second thoughts, since it's . . . for me."

I thought of Bonnie's gossip. It made me so ashamed of Arnold's Corners I was twice as determined to carry out my Big Idea.

"And I'm not joking, Rosalee, about the ten cents an hour. It would be taking advantage of you. Your parents will feel that you are wasting your time, I expect."

"They don't have to know," I said with a toss of my head. "It isn't polite to ask people how much they earn —Daddy said so."

41

Jenny's lips twitched. She got up and moved the hamburgers off the flame.

"In this particular case, they should know right from the beginning. Now—you'd better run along. And Rosalee—" she said as I started to leave the kitchen, "don't feel bad if they say no. I'll understand."

On the way home I made up Convincing Arguments. I would have to wait for the right moment to bring up the subject.

Mom did not ask as soon as I walked in the door whether I had gotten the job with Mr. Hooker. She had her mind on other things. Timmy was fussing and she was trying to get dinner ready. I swooped Timmy up in the air and took him out to play in the yard under the trees.

She called us in an hour and a half later. "I don't know why your daddy hasn't gotten here yet," she said, "but we won't wait. You may eat while I feed Timmy."

In a way I was relieved. It would be better to tell them both at the same time.

When we were through eating I helped clear the table and also dried the dishes without being asked. When I volunteered to give Timmy his bath and put him to bed, Mom gave me a sharp look.

"Rosalee Brigham, what have you done that you shouldn't?"

"Why, what do you mean? I haven't done anything I shouldn't!"

She was not convinced. "I've never known you to volunteer to work unless you wanted something or unless you needed forgiveness."

"Cross my heart!" I smote my chest—it is a grand gesture if you know how to do it. "You should expect the best of a person, or she may never change her ways."

"I'll be sure to remember that," Mom said dryly.

By the time Timmy was bathed and in his pajamas, he was too sleepy to wiggle. I sat in the rocking chair in his room and held him on my lap. He lay still in my arms while I sang to him. He does not make fun when I cannot quite reach the high notes. Soon he was asleep, but I did not put him in his crib right away. I thought of when this had been my room. The smell of pine drifted in through the window from the woods back of our house. The sounds of crickets and cheeping frogs had put me to sleep more nights than I could remember.

I felt sad and did not know why. Maybe it had something to do with that double-vision business—being in between little and grown-up. It is a noplace kind of place to be.

The noise of our pickup truck grinding into the driveway made me remember my promise to Jenny. But I still didn't get up. I listened to the rise and fall of Mom's and Daddy's voices in the kitchen. Once I heard them laugh loudly. Later I thought I heard Daddy's footsteps on the stairs. That was when, almost asleep myself, I put little old limp Timmy in his crib.

The bright lights of the kitchen hurt my eyes after being in the dark for so long. Mom was wiping the counter tops.

"Well," she said, "I thought you'd gone to sleep!"

"I almost did. Where's Daddy?"

"He's gone to bed—completely worn out. A shipment of feed came just as he was closing the store, and he had to help the driver unload the truck."

She pointed to my sombrero on the table. "He brought back your hat—on his head. You should have been here when he came in. He was a sight!"

I had to laugh, thinking of Daddy with my sombrero perched on top of his balding head, and the bingle balls dancing on the brim. I decided not to mention my Big Idea—yet. Tomorrow would be a better time to tell them both. I kissed Mom good night and went to my room.

5

✿✿✿✿✿✿✿✿✿✿✿

I woke up to the sound of Daddy's heavy footsteps trying to tiptoe and not doing a very good job of it. A few moments later I heard the whine of the pickup truck engine as it passed my window. The clock said six. Daddy would be back in an hour or so for breakfast.

I lay still for a few moments and listened to the early morning sounds coming through my open window. This time of day everything is fresh and new and not many cars are passing. The morning belongs to birds and bugs and little breezes. Sometimes I think people don't deserve morning—but still, I guess people get a lot of good things they do not deserve. When I go out into the morning, I feel quiet inside. It is better than church.

The minute hand had moved to five after. I jumped out of bed, threw the covers over the pillow, and pulled on my shorts and shirt. It wouldn't do to linger in bed today.

In the kitchen Daddy's coffee cup was turned upside

down on the drainboard. I grinned, imagining the expression on Mom's face when she came to cook breakfast and found I had beaten her to it. I looked around. Suddenly I saw our yellow kitchen—really saw it—for the first time.

It is like one you might see in a magazine—tile floor, built-in electric range, freezer stocked with enough food to feed the entire community, washing machine, electric dryer. I had taken these things for granted for as long as I could remember. But now I was remembering Jenny's kitchen, comparing it to ours.

I guess I was thinking about Jenny so hard that I didn't realize I was banging plates and clunking silver until I came face-to-face with Mom in the doorway, sleepy-eyed and wrapped in her housecoat.

"Could you be a little quieter?" she said. "I heard you all the way upstairs, with the door closed."

"Sorry," I muttered. "Would you like your egg fried or scrambled?"

"I'll take it scrambled lightly, now that you ask," she said, looking around. "My! I won't have to do a thing, will I?"

She sat at her place, and I finished fixing our breakfast. "You did that like a professional," she said when I set the two full plates on the table.

"Anybody could do a professional job with all this equipment," I said with a wave of the hand. "The true test would be if you could do it all with muscle and elbow grease."

Mom raised her eyebrows and took a bite of toast.

"Some people do," I went on, still thinking of Jenny.

"I suppose so," she said, but she didn't sound interested. "What do you say to our going over to Bent City today? We could spend the whole day. We haven't done that since Timmy was born."

I stopped chewing. My heart scooted all the way down to my toes. "I don't know," I hedged. "It wouldn't be much fun with Timmy along."

"Oh, I didn't mean take him along. Maybe Jenny Chapman would keep him. Her baby is about his age and she could use the money, I'm sure."

"No!" I shouted. Mom gave me a funny look. I realized that I had been too forceful about it. "I mean . . . I dropped by for a minute yesterday and she had so much sewing to do—why, she doesn't even have time to read!"

Mom's face began closing up. "Lots of people don't have time to read," she said. "If you don't want to go, it's all right with me. I just thought you'd like a change."

But she was disappointed, I could tell. She got up from the table and carried the dirty dishes to the sink. I wasn't hungry anymore, but I kept eating and wished that I hadn't gotten out of bed so early.

It was time to tell her about my job with Jenny. I was making up the words when Daddy arrived for breakfast, and somehow all the words I made up just flew out of my head. I escaped to my room. If I didn't tell them soon, Daddy would go to Jenny's to ask her to keep Timmy—and she would know that I had not mentioned the Big Idea to my folks. She would think I thought the same things about her that everybody else in Arnold's Corners does.

Daddy tapped on the door and stuck his head in.

"What's this about you not wanting to go to Bent City?"

"It just isn't what I want to do today, that's all."

"You ought to think about other people's feelings once in a while, Rosalee." He lowered his voice. "A day off would do your mother a world of good. She'd get a kick out of going shopping with you."

"I suppose it doesn't matter whether I want to go or not." I did not mean to be sassy, but it came out that way.

He gave me an extra stern look. "Right!" he snapped.

"Now—" he went on in a normal tone of voice, "I'll stop by Jenny Chapman's on the way back to the store—"

"No," I said, folding my arms. "I tried to tell Mom. It isn't fair to ask Jenny to keep Timmy when she has all her other work to do and Ruthie to care for besides. You can't sew and look after two little kids. I won't go if Jenny has to keep Timmy."

Mom's face appeared beside Daddy's in the doorway. "Don't worry! Neither of us will go. If I'd known there was going to be such a fuss, I'd never have brought it up, believe me." Her footsteps marched away. Daddy gave me a look that said, Now you've gone and done it, and he left too.

Usually I get into trouble by talking too much—this time it was from not talking enough. I should have told Mom about Jenny as soon as I got home the night before. I should have explained about Ruthie rolling off the porch and having to stay in the playpen the whole, hot day. Having Timmy, Mom would have understood. It is always easy to see, too late, what you should have done.

I heard her footsteps coming down the stairs and Timmy's morning crow. So I took a deep breath and walked out to face the music. It was plain from the look on her face that she was still peeved.

"Well," she said, "do you think you might be available to help me today?"

"Yes," I said. My chest was heavy inside. "Mom—"

Mom went on down the hall to the kitchen. "What is it?"

"I want to explain something," I said, following close behind. "From the very beginning to the very end."

"You'll have to do it while I feed Timmy. I can't drop everything to sit and listen."

I sat in a chair and waited until she had Timmy's breakfast ready and had strapped him into his high chair. Then I told her about the day before, and how I had planned to go to Jenny's to help out.

"Why didn't you say so?" she asked when I had finished.

"I was going to tell you and Daddy at the same time," I said. "Jenny said I had to ask you both. But there was never a good—"

"Actually, I'm surprised at Jenny," Mom interrupted, spooning egg into Timmy's open mouth. "She should know there's plenty for you to do around here."

I started getting tight inside. You have to be so careful when you are talking to grown-ups. "It was my idea," I said. "I suggested it. She told me she couldn't pay more than ten cents an hour—that's what I told her I'd work for—and she said that would be taking advantage of me."

"I quite agree," said Mom.

"But she needs somebody! I'd do it for nothing if she'd let me."

"While I'm paying someone else a dollar an hour to keep Timmy?"

"I would never go when you needed me to keep Timmy. She made me promise. If you say no, she won't let me do it at all."

Except for Timmy's bare feet drumming against the high chair and his smacking noises while he chewed soggy toast, the kitchen was very quiet for what seemed like an age.

"Rosalee, I'm proud of you for wanting to help Jenny. I think it's very fine—"

I shook my head. She was missing the whole point. "It isn't so fine. I don't need money—not even the ten cents an hour. I have you and Daddy to look after me. I have everything I need."

"I haven't finished," Mom said sharply. "It isn't our fault that Jenny lives the way she does. We don't know anything about her, really. Frankly I don't like the idea of your going over there every day."

All of a sudden I was so mad I couldn't hold in any more. "You wouldn't say that if I told you I'd be earning a dollar an hour, would you?" I yelled. "You'd let me do most anything for a dollar an hour and call it honest work!"

I should not have started hollering, because I started crying. I couldn't help it. I got up and ran to my room. Mom called me a couple of times but I pretended not to hear. Timmy began to cry. I lay down across my bed and put the pillow over my head to shut out noises, but I could still hear the clock ticking. I did not want to see what time it was.

I do not know how long I lay there, mad at myself for letting everything get out of control—just like a baby. What would Mr. King think if he could see me now? Wise. Phooey!

Then I heard Mom's voice from the doorway.

"Rosalee—"

It was hot under the pillow. My eyes burned and my nose was stopped up. "What?" I mumbled.

"Get up and wash your face. You can't go to Jenny's looking like that."

I thought I was hearing things. I jumped up and flung off the pillow. "You mean you're going to let me go? After how I acted and what I said?"

Mom's eyes looked a little pink around the edges. She lifted her chin. "I'm willing for you to try it out, so long as it doesn't interfere with your work at home, or at the store."

I was across the room in one leap, and I hugged her so hard she gasped for breath. "Oh, Mom, thanks! I'll work hard. I'll do anything you say. Just tell me ahead of time so I can plan!"

"Don't worry," she said. She gave me an uncertain pat on the shoulder. "You'll be notified."

6

❀❀❀❀❀❀❀❀❀❀❀

The two dimes in my pocket made a thin little jingle as I walked home from Jenny's at noon that day. I could have earned twenty cents in a few minutes of sweeping the store. Some things, though, are worth more than money. It wasn't so much what I had done as what Jenny had been able to do because I was there to look after Ruthie. That is what I mean by an honest day's work.

And it was work, let me tell you. Baby-sitting is a very exhausting experience, especially if you are working for somebody else and know you have to be responsible for your own mistakes. As far as wild babies are concerned, Ruthie runs Timmy a close race, even if she is a girl. It is probably due to the fact she's stayed penned up so much that she has a lot of excess energy.

I recognized the particular sound of our pickup truck engine coming along the road behind me. Shortly Daddy pulled up beside me.

"Want a ride, lady?"

"Yes," I said, "but my father does not like me to ride with strangers."

"O.K.," he answered, shifting gears as though to take off again. "Someday we'll have to get ourselves introduced. Looks like it may start raining after a while."

I looked up at the sky. Sure enough, dark clouds were piling up in the southwest. I took a running jump and landed in the back of the truck with a number of fertilizer-smelling sacks and an assortment of tools.

"Drive on, Jeeves!" I called, but he had already started without the order. In no time we were rolling into our driveway.

"You didn't show up at the store this morning," he said as he helped me down from the truck.

"I have a job," I said.

"When did this come about? Why doesn't anybody tell me anything?"

I told him about my first morning's work and how Jenny had been able to finish one dress and start another because I kept Ruthie out of mischief. I did not dwell upon Mom's halfhearted permission, as I was sure he would learn about that soon enough. He did not say much one way or the other—didn't even ask how much I was earning—but I had a good idea what he was thinking. There was that same twitch of his jaw I had seen when he told me what he thought of my visiting May.

Mom had not recovered from our fuss that morning. She looked tired. She had cooked a huge meal—roast, brown gravy, biscuits, vegetables, pie, and all. My heart sank. She only cooks big meals in the middle of the day when she is feeling sorry for herself. She had already fed Timmy and put him to bed for his afternoon nap.

"How was your job this morning?" she asked as we began to eat.

"Fine," I said.

There was a lot of chewing and clanking of silverware on plates for the next few minutes. I had made up my mind to be seen and not heard. Then Daddy said, "Too bad you weren't at the store. Your Indian friend came in and paid up today."

I raised my eyebrows and gave him what I hoped was a cool glance. "Oh, you mean Mr. King?"

"Yes," said Daddy. "How many Indian friends do you have?"

I twisted my mouth at him. Sometimes he thinks he is so cute.

"As a matter of fact," he went on, "I cashed a check for him—right large amount, too, from North Carolina State University. However, the check didn't say what he was being paid *for*. I looked. I asked him was he a student at the university—to be polite. I have heard of these fringe characters that claim to be students but just hang around to start trouble."

Mom was looking puzzled. She did not know about Mr. King.

Daddy went right on talking. "He said to me, 'Well, I suppose you could call me a student. I learn something new every day.' How's that for a backhanded answer?"

"Who is he?" Mom broke in.

"Ask Rosalee, there," Daddy said. "She's his pal, not me."

"Daddy is being silly," I said. "I don't know any more about the gentleman than he does, but I'm not willing to make a bad judgment of him just because he's a stranger!" I told Mom about him, but I didn't mention my copper highlights, as I did not think she would be interested.

"I don't know what he's doing here," I finished, "and I'll be the last to ask. I can't see why anyone would come to Arnold's Corners unless it was an absolute emergency, but it seems to me that as long as you know his word is good and that he pays his debts, that's all you need to be concerned about!"

Daddy put his napkin beside his plate, stood, and hitched up his pants. "When I want to hear a sermon on a weekday, I'll go visit the preacher," he said, giving me an offended look. "And if you don't watch your tongue, I will begin to think that who you associate with is having a bad effect on you. Now—do I need to be looking around for new help at the store since you have a job elsewhere?"

"I'll be there," I said. "It is part of the bargain. I'm not to work for Jenny if you or Mom need me worse than she does."

"Well, I'm glad to hear you are giving your family some consideration," Daddy said. He kissed Mom good-by and went back to the store.

"You hurt his feelings," she told me when the two of us were alone.

"I didn't mean to," I said. "It isn't just Daddy—it's everybody in this whole community. Always making snap judgments. . . ."

"Well," she said, picking up her dishes, "it depends on your point of view. You are certainly making your share of them today!"

A loud clap of thunder kept me from answering, which was probably good, since I have a tendency to say the wrong thing in an argument. Timmy woke from his nap and set up a howl. While Mom went to get him,

55

I ran around closing windows against the rain. When the lightning and thunder stopped and the storm had settled into a steady summer drizzle, I left for the store.

I must admit I did not go with a cheerful attitude, knowing the store was going to be a mess. When it rains, the men in Arnold's Corners congregate there to yak. Well, not all of them—just those you'd as soon do without. You'd think they would make more constructive use of their time.

There were several cars and trucks parked around the front of the store—if anybody wanted to buy a tank of gasoline he couldn't get close enough. Anyhow, it wasn't likely. Daddy had put up a sign just over the gas pump that said No CREDIT CARDS. I suppose he did not want to go through the same embarrassment he had just experienced with Mr. King, but I could not help feeling that he was going to lose a lot of beach-bound customers this summer.

"Hey, Red!" Casey Small hollered as soon as I walked in. "Where'd you get that carrot top?"

"I inherited it from my father," I said in my cool business voice.

It is disgusting. He says the exact same thing every time he sees me. Suddenly I thought about Mr. King, and I said, "My hair isn't red, actually. It's auburn with copper highlights."

Bill Steed's mouth dropped open. "What kind of headlights?"

Everybody laughed at my expense. They don't want to get on the bad side of Bill Steed. He is fat, tall, broad, and freckled, with oily black hair. He is easily irritated. I was sorry I had opened my mouth.

"Forget it," I said. I went behind the counter to get a clean cloth and the Windex bottle. I stayed there until the men had forgotten me and had gone on to their usual dull topics—cars, crops, and politics.

Daddy came out of the stock room. "Didn't think you'd bother after the rain came," he said to me, raising his voice so as to be heard above the noisy conversation.

I made a face. "It is a waste of time, but I will polish the showcases."

Daddy looked grim. He doesn't like the muddied floors with squashed cigarette butts and scattered soda bottles any better than I do. "Do the best you can," was all he said. "I'm in the stock room if anybody needs me."

I kept an eye on the men while I worked, which wasn't hard to do even when my back was turned. I could see their reflections in the showcases as I polished. Besides Bill and Casey, there were the Hawkins twins, Elmer and Carson. They are nearly forty years old and look so much alike that nobody has ever been able to tell which is which, except their own mother. Mr. Les Barton sat on top of the ice-cream cabinet drinking Pepsi, while his three half-grown sons propped themselves against whatever they could find that would hold them up.

The only chair Daddy has in the store was occupied by Mr. Purdy Brown, who is a deacon in the Mt. Pisgah Baptist Church and won the prize for being the oldest daddy on Father's Day last year, being eighty-seven. I like Mr. Purdy. He is old enough so he does not have to bow down to anybody, especially Bill Steed. Mr. Purdy has retired from farming, but he likes to talk crops with everybody. He comes to the store every afternoon that he feels like walking the mile from his house. I hope when I am eighty-seven I will still feel like walking a mile, but I also hope I will do it for something more inspiring.

All of a sudden, I realized that the store was perfectly quiet, except for the squeak of my polishing rag on glass. I whirled around. They were all in their same places but every face was closed and distrustful. Every eye was turned toward the front door.

My heart flopped. Mr. King stood there. With his long hair and mustache, he was a spectacle, sure enough. Just for a moment, I thought, Why did you have to come in here now and start trouble by being so different in front of everybody? But then I was ashamed. I set the Windex bottle on top of the counter with a loud bang that made everybody's eyes blink.

"Well, howdy!" I sang out. "You came at just the right time! Let me introduce you to some of Arnold's Corners' hardworking citizens." I was sure Mr. King got the full sarcasm of that remark, but he did not let on. I led him over to them, introduced him all around, and called every person by name—except I got Elmer and Carson mixed up, of course. Mr. King offered his hand, which they were obliged to shake. Mr. Purdy struggled to get up and offer Mr. King his chair, but Mr. King gently urged him to keep it. I could have hugged them both. At least there were two gentlemen in the group.

Mr. King was very friendly, but he was in hostile territory. I racked my brain for some way to sweeten the atmosphere.

"What can I do for you this afternoon?" I asked. I hoped, for his sake, that he'd buy something and leave.

"Nothing, really," he said, cheerful as you please. He found himself a place to lean on the ice-cream cabinet. Mr. Les Barton moved in the other direction as far as he could without falling off. "Thought I'd nose around a bit and get better acquainted, since I'm going to be here a while."

I resigned myself then to the fact that a girl my age is not meant to defend a full-grown man of the world, unless you count Pocahontas and John Smith, which is a story I am inclined to doubt. Mr. King did not seem ill at ease, which made me feel some better about abandoning him to the wolves.

I have read in books that a psychologist gets his patients to start talking by just sitting until the silence becomes unbearable and somebody *has* to say something. It is hardly ever the psychologist who gives in. Maybe Mr. King has read that too. At any rate, it did not bother him that the men were stony quiet. He leaned and waited, cocking his head to one side like he was studying them all very carefully. Sure enough, Bill Steed straightened up and said in a loud voice, "You say you plan to stay here a while?"

Mr. King nodded. "I hope to."

They all considered this possibility. "Where you puttin' up at?" asked Mr. Barton.

"I have a camper. Mr. Lyman Hayes is letting me stay on his place."

Mr. Barton nodded, as though that explained everything.

"You must've come right far," Mr. Purdy Brown said. He is a great respecter of distances, having been born in a time when people did not travel far or fast. "We don't hardly ever see men with so much hair, except on the television."

Mr. King did not take offense. "I didn't come so far. From State University, as a matter of fact."

"You ain't no student," Bill said.

"Well, no. At least not anymore. I . . . work there now."

"Oh? Doing what?"

"Painting."

I am ashamed to admit that I was listening to the conversation with as much curiosity as the three Barton boys, although I did have the good manners not to stand with my mouth open the way they were doing. When Mr. King said his work was painting, I was as astonished as anybody. I tried to picture him in white coveralls and hat. It was the most unlikely thing I could think of, and yet he did not seem the type to tell a straight-out fib.

"You mean, like houses and walls?" Mr. Barton wondered. "I do some of that myself, from time to time. Good-paying work."

"Yes, it pays pretty well," Mr. King said solemnly. The men looked him up and down. The mean air seemed to give a little.

"You come here for your vacation, I guess," Casey said.

"Well . . . ," said Mr. King. "You could say that—but I still have some walls to do when I get back."

It was a puzzling statement. I thought he must be in great demand, if they'd let him off for a vacation right in the middle of a job.

Bill rubbed his beefy hands together. "I guess you might as well know that folks in Arnold's Corners don't go for all that long hair and drug stuff," he said. "We're plain around here. We don't like outsiders trying to start something."

I could have clobbered him, I was so mortified. "Bill Steed, you don't have any right to speak for Arnold's Corners!" I exclaimed. "Mr. King isn't likely to cause near the trouble you cause when you get up of a morning!"

My daddy elected to come out of the back room just in time to hear me utter those immortal words.

Bill's face turned brick red. Casey sucked in his breath. Mr. Purdy regarded me with interest. Bill's eyes blazed out at me and then toward Daddy in the back of the store.

"You hear that, Tal?" he hollered. "You hear your girl sass me?"

Daddy moved toward the front. I had never seen him so grim. "What's the trouble here?" he said gruffly.

"Mr. Steed said some very insulting things to Mr. King," I said, making my voice sound firm. I would not cry in front of Bill Steed if he drove spikes under my fingernails. "I thought it was rude to speak so to someone who has been nothing but friendly!"

"I did not insult this—this hippie!" Bill shouted. "I told him something I thought he ought to know. A friendly warning is what I gave him. And you, Miss Smarty-Mouth, you ought to have your teeth scrubbed with lye soap, talking the way you have talked to me!"

"All right now, hold on there, Bill," Daddy said. "She's only a girl. I don't guess she meant to upset you."

I had to bite my tongue to keep from saying yes, I did mean to. Daddy was on the spot because of me, and I had to help him even if I denied my principles.

All this time Mr. King had been standing by looking puzzled and embarrassed. "I'll be going," he said in a low voice. "Glad to have met all of you." Nobody tried to stop him, not even Daddy.

"Don't forget what I told you!" Bill called after him. "Maybe Miss Redhead don't think I speak for Arnold's

Corners, but maybe she don't know everything either!"

There was absolute silence inside the store, except for Bill's puffing breath. We heard the camper motor start up and listened until the engine noise was lost in the distance. Then Daddy said in a voice of steel, "Get out of here, Bill Steed, and don't ever let me see you in this store again until you learn some manners!"

It was Bill's turn to be astounded. I would have laughed out loud, only I was too scared. Bill Steed is not somebody to mess around with.

"Sure, Tal, I'll go," Bill said, trying to act smooth, but he was humiliated and mad, and I knew he wasn't likely to forget this day. "We'll all go, won't we boys?"

The others looked sideways at one another.

"I haven't invited anybody else out," Daddy said.

Bill ignored him. "Well—aren't you coming? Are you going to stay around here in a store that patronizes trash?"

To a man they started moving toward the door, except for Mr. Purdy, who said, "I'm not done sittin' here."

When they were gone, Daddy turned on his heel and headed for the stock room once more. I followed him.

"I'm sorry," I said. "I just couldn't stand his meanness."

"I wish you picked your friends with more care!" Daddy snapped. I could see then how upset he was. The muscle in his jaw twitched furiously. He wiped at his face with his hand, which was shaking. "If you've got any influence over that Mr. King, ask him not to come here again. I don't want any trouble, the Lord knows. Once Bill gets through shooting off his mouth, I'll be lucky if I'm still in business."

7

❁❁❁❁❁❁❁❁❁❁❁❁

It was not necessary for me to exert my influence over Mr. King. He did not come back to Brigham's Store.

I have heard of people who, when they were troubled, buried themselves in their work. With my three jobs I certainly had plenty of work to bury myself in. The ten Bookmobile books moldered on my night table like John Brown's body in his grave. It was not a very fulfilling kind of life, but I found out what Jenny Chapman was up against trying to make a living at sewing and altering.

Thanks to Mom, who worked in a dress shop in Bent City before she was married and is an expert on ladies' clothes, I have learned more than I care to know on the subject. She tells me that finished seams, bound buttonholes, linings, matched patterns, monograms, and trim are the things that make a dress expensive. That was the sort of dress Jenny turned out for her customers. It took at least a day to make one.

I was playing with Ruthie in Jenny's front room the Friday that Mrs. Hooker came by to pick up a dress she had ordered. Even I thought it was pretty, and I do not pay attention to clothes. But she hardly looked at the dress Jenny held up for inspection.

"How much do I owe you?" Mrs. Hooker wanted to know.

"Four dollars," answered Jenny.

I could not believe my ears. Four dollars! It could easily bring thirty or forty at the Exclusive Shoppe in Bent City!

Mrs. Hooker was astounded too, but for different reasons.

"Four dollars did you say? Well, for goodness' sake! I bought the material and the pattern—I didn't have any idea it would cost four dollars to have it made. Why, I would've run it up myself if I'd known you'd charge that much—I was only trying to save myself some time. Do you realize I paid close to nine dollars for that material? It's a mighty simple-looking pattern, seems to me."

"It's simple-looking," Jenny said when Mrs. Hooker stopped to take a breath, "but I had to alter the pattern quite a bit—and the lines are complicated."

"Well, I guess I'll have to pay for it, now you've made it," Mrs. Hooker interrupted. "One thing for sure, nobody but me can wear it!"

She was certainly right about that. Mrs. Hooker is as tall and long-legged as her husband is short and fat. Where he resembles a goldfish, she is more like a conger eel.

Neither Jenny nor I said a word until we heard Mrs. Hooker's car engine cough, rattle, and catch. I guess

Jenny saw how angry I felt because she said, "I don't let her bother me."

It bothered me plenty. I did some calculating. How could she, at her rates, make enough money to support Ruthie and herself? I worried about it all the rest of the day. Then I dreamed that night that the twenty cents Jenny had given me at noon was her last penny.

"My, you're up early!" Mom said when I came to the kitchen the next morning. "This is Saturday. You could sleep late." When I did not answer, she said, "You aren't planning to baby-sit for Jenny today, are you?"

"No, ma'am," I mumbled. The stack of pancakes she set in front of me smelled delicious, but I was not very hungry somehow.

"You should be around girls your own age."

"Yeah," I said. "I thought I might ride around on my bike—see who's out."

"You and Bonnie Lewis used to be such good friends."

I did not reply to that. Mothers and daughters have different ideas about friends.

I went out after breakfast like I knew where I was going, but once on my bike I had to admit that I couldn't think of a soul who would welcome my coming. That is not a very good feeling.

Rain had made the road squashy, and my bike was old—a victim of having been left out in the elements too many times. Two miles later, exhausted from pedaling so constantly—you can't coast in mud—I swallowed my pride. It was about all I could swallow at that point, as I had a very dry mouth. I decided to pedal forty times more. Then I would stop, get off the bike, check the chain and the tires, and maybe shake my head a little—in case anyone might be watching. After that I would turn around and go home. It was a relief to make the decision, even though I was having to face the fact that I had no place to go and no friends to meet.

Pedaling forty times put me around a curve and smack in front of May Thomas' house. Bud was sitting astraddle the barn-lot gate.

"Hey, Rosalee!" someone shouted. "You come to ride Baby Doll?"

I looked up to see May making a flying leap from the front porch. "I've been hopin' you'd come," she panted, running out to the road through the barnyard. Chickens and cats scattered ahead of her.

"I was just riding around," I said, remembering what Daddy said about coming to May's. "It's probably time I went home."

May's face fell. I thought about what I had been wishing for since I got up that morning.

"But I believe I'll stay."

May jumped in the air and yelled like a cheerleader. "I'll bet you're perishing of thirst," she said. "Come on —I'll get you some water."

Well, I *was* thirsty, and it certainly would not be polite to let May bring water all the way to the road. I leaned my bike against the mailbox and followed her to the house.

May's mother was standing just inside the screen door. I had seen her only once before, at the school Christmas play. Ed stood beside her. His head barely came to her waist.

"Hey," I said, and bobbed my head.

"May's got to help me with the ironing today," Mrs. Thomas said flatly.

My face began to burn. It was not my intention to cause trouble. Girls and mothers have a hard enough time getting along as it is.

"Yes, ma'am," I said, backing down the steps. "I will come another time."

"I invited Rosalee to come and ride Baby Doll," May said, drawing herself up to full height, which is, as you know, considerable. "I have just this second offered her some water because she has come all the way from her house on her bicycle in the hot sun!" For a long minute she and her mother just looked at each other. I wished I were twenty miles away. I gazed in the other direction and wondered if I should say anything.

Mrs. Thomas cleared her throat. "You can bring her a drink of water. And I reck'n you can play for a while till I'm ready for you. But you better not go off!" She turned and went away through the house. Ed lingered a second longer and grinned at me, then he disappeared too.

"I could help you with the work," I said.

May made a face. "There's not all that much to do. Wait in the swing. I'll get your water."

She brought it in a bumpy yellow glass. It tasted sweet and I drank it every bit without taking a breath.

"Now," she said, setting the glass on the windowsill, "let's see who gets to the barn first!"

The warm, dark animal smell inside the barn burned my nose. Baby Doll swung her head around and snuffled my hand.

"She still remembers that cookie you gave her." May grinned as she hauled the bridle down from a peg on the wall. "You made a friend for life."

"I'd like that," I said, rubbing the pony's soft nose.

"Not many friends are for life—or even for a few months, as far as that goes."

"Yeah."

We looked at each other across Baby Doll's back. Neither of us said anything else on the subject, but I did not feel lonesome anymore.

Bud was waiting for us when we came out into the sunlight. He is one grade higher than us in school. He is also tall and lean, like May, but seems not so strong-looking.

"Where you going?" he asked.

"To ride," said May. She led Baby Doll right on past him.

"I mean *where*?"

"I don't know that it's any of your business!"

"Are you going down the woods path?"

"We might."

"You'll be sorry if you do!"

May stopped in her tracks and turned on him with her feet apart and her hands on her hips. "I'd like to know why? What you going to do about it?"

"I'll tell Mama. You know what she said about those hippies in the woods."

A worried look flitted through May's eyes, but her voice didn't waver. "You're just talkin' like that 'cause you don't want me to show Rosalee the creek!" she said. "And you don't need to tell Mama anything, because if you do, won't neither of us—you *or* me—get to go there ever again. So you better mind your mouth!"

Bud muttered something and stalked off toward the barn.

"What's this about hippies in the woods?" I asked. I stumbled along on Baby Doll's other side. "In Arnold's *Corners?*"

68

"Well, I don't especially believe it," May said, "but Mama heard there was a long-hair character stonkin' around back in the woods. She won't hardly let us get out of her sight since she heard it."

"What in the world would hippies be doing in Arnold's Corners?" I asked. "Would you come here from someplace else?"

May looked at me for a moment, then broke out laughing. "No. No, I sure wouldn't!"

She made me get on the pony's back, saying she could ride anytime. There was no saddle, just a feed sack draped across. She went ahead, the dust of the field path puffing up and coating her dark legs with gray. Baby Doll and I followed at a walk. It was a sleepy day. The wind rustled through the new cornstalk leaves in the field. I could not remember feeling so contented since I was born.

"I hardly see you, now school is out," May said over her shoulder.

"I'm keeping Jenny Chapman's baby two hours a morning and working at the store afternoons, and looking after Timmy, and helping Mom the rest of the time." I sighed. "I don't even have time to think."

"I wish I had a job looking after babies instead of working in tobacco," May said. "I love babies. When I grow up I intend to work where there's lots of them."

The woods began at the back of the cornfield. The path we were on kept right on going, but instead of being dirt it was covered here with pine needles and layers of decayed leaves. Baby Doll lifted her head and snorted.

"She likes it here," May said, smiling back at her pony. "She and Bud and me come down here a lot—"

The words were not out of her mouth when Baby

Doll veered off the path and began to run. The next thing I knew, we had galloped past May and I was about to fall off.

"Hold on tight!" May hollered from somewhere behind us. I did not need that piece of advice, as I was trying to keep my head from being knocked off by low-hanging tree branches. For the moment it seemed like a waste of time to wonder why a perfectly gentle pony should go crashing off into the woods like a wild bull.

The land began to slope, at first gradually and then more sharply. I felt as helpless as the time I went on a roller coaster at the State Fair. "Please, Baby Doll!" I pleaded close to her ear. "Slow down!"

She stopped so suddenly I almost went over her head. I sat up—and gawked. I could not believe I was still in Arnold's Corners. I was looking at a picture post card, except that it was alive and moving. Summer rains had filled the creek bed and now water bubbled over rocks and tree stumps. Huge boulders lined the bank on each side.

"It's my favorite spot in the whole world," May said breathlessly as she came running up. "Bud and me found it last spring, after Pa moved us to Mr. Lewis' farm. We never told anybody else about it—never seen anybody else here, either. See that tall rock on the other side? That's where we have picnics sometimes. We never been beyond it, though."

The high rock jutted over the creek. Black and moss-covered, its top disappeared in a thicket of weeds and bushes.

"Gosh!" I said. "I bet that rock was here before the Indians came!" I got down from Baby Doll's back and fastened her lead line to a small tree. My knees were wobbly.

"Let's wade!" May was rolling up the legs of her jeans. I did not need to be begged. We stepped into the icy water at the same time, and both of us squealed.

I held up a hand. "Silence! Indians lurk in yonder woods."

May snorted. "Or hippies."

We giggled like a couple of goons as we waded back and forth to get used to the cold.

Suddenly there was a tremendous crashing through the brush on the far side. Stones rattled and tumbled from the top of the jutting rock, splashing around us into the creek.

Baby Doll whinnied. May shrieked. Someone tall and dark stepped out of the bushes onto the rock above.

8

✿✿✿✿✿✿✿✿✿✿✿✿

That was the longest second of my life, with May and me up to our knees in cold creek water, too scared to move, and some strange giant about to leap upon us from above. I could not even yell for help.

The giant stepped closer to the edge of the rock and peered over at us. The sun fell across his face. It was Mr. King.

"Well, well—Lady Rose of the Auburn Locks!" he called down in his usual friendly way. You would never have thought that only a few days before he had been humiliated in my own daddy's store.

May and I looked at each other. I wondered if my eyes were as wide and dark as hers. My heart began to thump again—twice as hard, to make up for lost time.

"It's me all right," I said, and my voice sounded strangled. I swallowed and tried again. "You sure can sneak up on people! May and I thought that we and Baby Doll were the only people within miles."

Mr. King shaded his eyes and looked around. "Baby Doll?"

"There," I said, pointing to the pony. "That's Baby Doll. This is May Thomas."

Mr. King threw back his head and laughed so loudly it echoed in the treetops.

"He's a hippie, ain't he?" May whispered.

"No! That's Mr. King," I whispered back. "He does . . . did business at our store until . . . a few days ago."

"So!" he said finally. "You and May and Baby Doll are the only people around? Well, I must say that Baby Doll has the longest nose. I'm happy to meet you, May." He smiled down at us.

May grinned back. The fright went out of her eyes.

"How did you find this place?" I asked.

He pointed to the woods behind him. "It isn't lost. Mr. Hayes owns the property and I have free run of it so long as I don't burn down the timber or throw trash in the water. This rock I'm standing on is part of the landscape. A person could walk right off it without realizing until too late. It's quite ancient—been here millions of years."

"That's what I thought!" I exclaimed.

"Oh? Why did you think so?" He slithered easily down the rock. He sat on the creek bank, slipped off his shoes, and rolled up his trouser legs. He had on a pair of old paint-splashed denims that made him resemble a walking rainbow.

"I don't know," I said. "It just feels old. We'd just been talking about Indians and when you stepped out—"

"—you thought you'd been ambushed," he finished,

wading into the water. He did not even flinch at the chill.

"How'd you know?" May breathed.

"We Indians know all sorts of things." He grinned.

"Are you really an Indian?" I began and bit my tongue. What an Arnold's Corners thing to say!

"Part Cherokee," he said, not in the least offended. "I brag about it a lot."

May and I looked at each other, and we both started laughing. We have met plenty of bragging people in Berry County, but not a single soul that would admit to it—especially grown-ups!

"Bud and me never saw anybody here before," May said when we quit giggling. "We come here nearly every day we aren't working in tobacco." She swished her foot back and forth in the water and looked down at the ripples she had made. "We sort of hoped we were the only ones knew about it. But I guess that was crazy—land has to belong to somebody . . ."

"Don't worry," Mr. King said. "Your secret's safe with me, and with Mr. Hayes too. He doesn't want a bunch of picnickers invading his territory, and I certainly don't. Some of the archaeologists think there was a large Indian settlement in this area of the state. I wouldn't be surprised if this were the very spot."

The three of us stood in the stream and listened to the forest noises—the rushing water, the wind in the treetops, and the birds. I could almost see tepees and campfires along the bank!

I discovered that day why grown-ups like conversation. We sat on the rocks along the creek bank and covered nearly every subject of importance under the sun, including families, and respect of people's opinions, and war, and work. It was very enlightening.

74

Mr. King was interested in anything we had to tell about Arnold's Corners, if you can imagine it. He asked about school and how we liked it, and what we thought about this and that. As I have mentioned before, I have not often been asked by a grown-up for my opinions. It sort of goes to your head.

Mr. King, for his part, told us stories of places he had been. Although I have read in books about Denmark, Iceland, Switzerland, Japan, France, and Italy, I have never met a person who has been to them all. It was on the tip of my tongue to ask him why, when he had been to so many splendid countries of the world, he was spending his summer vacation in such a place as Arnold's Corners.

But I could not bring myself to ask. If I'm going to get Arnold's Corners out of my system, I have got to learn that people will give out information about themselves when they are ready to trust you with it.

"It is just as well," I told him, "that you are asking May and me about Arnold's Corners. You'd never know, from talking to other folks around here, whether you'd learned anything true. People make up stuff."

Mr. King put his head to one side and looked at me hard. "Why do you suppose they feel they need to make up stories?"

"I know the answer to that," May spoke up. She poked with a stick at a snail half buried in the mud. "It's because what is true is so plain."

"You've probably got it exactly right," Mr. King chuckled. He fished in his pocket, took out a handful of foil-wrapped toffees, and divided them equally among us. "But, you know, what's true doesn't have to be plain and dull—you don't have to travel all over the world to live an exciting life."

75

"That's easy for you to say," I told him, "because you don't have to stay in Arnold's Corners like we do."

"Yeah," May nodded. "And Rosalee and me are going away forever, soon as we're old enough."

"Too bad for Arnold's Corners," Mr. King sighed, standing up and stretching his long arms over his head. "Maybe you'll change your mind—forever's a very long time."

"Things would have to change a lot to make me change *my* mind," I muttered. I was about to ask him how you could live an exciting life without going out into the world to seek your fortune when he looked at his watch and then at the sun.

"Say, I wonder if you two girls would do me a favor?"

May and I looked at each other.

"Wait here," he said, before we could answer. "I'll be right back."

He splashed through the creek to the other side. We watched him scramble up the rock and listened to his footsteps crunching off into the woods.

"What you reckon he wants?" May asked.

I felt a tad uneasy. I tried to imagine explaining our morning to Mom or Mrs. Thomas. I could tell from the frown on May's face that she was thinking along the same lines.

"We ought to have a signal," I said. "If I think it's O.K., I'll scratch my head, and if you agree, you do the same. We've both got to agree."

Mr. King was soon back, carrying under his arm what looked to be a huge writing tablet with no lines. His shirt pocket was full of pencils.

"I've been wanting to sketch someone in this background, but I couldn't bring myself to tell anyone about the place. Now you're here, the problem is solved —that is, if you'll agree to sit rather still on that flat rock for about thirty minutes . . ."

May and I scratched heads at the same time. After all, we didn't want anybody else to know about the place, either!

I did not know that sitting still was so hard. Mr. King had us turned toward each other on the rock, but we were supposed to look at the creek. He told me to let my braids hang down in front. May had to hold a stick in her hand and pretend to poke in the water. We giggled a lot and tried not to think about itching or getting numb.

He sat on the opposite bank and worked. We couldn't see him without looking sideways, but his pencil flew all over the big tablet. He talked to himself for the entire thirty minutes, which seems like three hours when you cannot move.

"There!" he said, with one last flourish of the pencil. "You may move."

May and I groaned.

"My fingers are plumb stiff from holding that stick so long," she said. She tossed it into the creek and dusted her hands together. "Do we get to see the picture?"

"Of course!" He waded across and held the sketch for us to see. It was May and me, all right, plain as anything—stick, braids, and all.

"Gosh!" May stared. "That's right good!"

"Yeah," I agreed. "It isn't bad at all. Do you do this kind of thing much?"

"Well—whenever I have time," he said. His eyes were crinkled at the corners the way Daddy's are when he is about to laugh. I wondered what the joke was.

"And speaking of time," he went on, "it's nearly

twelve o'clock. If your mothers are expecting you for lunch, you'd better start back soon."

May's hand flew to her mouth. "Glory be! Mama's going to beat the stuffin's out of me!"

We turned and scrambled up the bank toward Baby Doll. "You ride this time," I said. "I'll follow. You'd better get home as quick as you can!"

We were in such a hurry I almost forgot Mr. King. When I looked back to wave good-by to him, he had already disappeared.

May swung up onto Baby Doll's back and urged the pony to a trot up the slope. Over and over she said, "What am I going to tell Mama?"

"You can blame it on me," I said, struggling up the hill behind her. "Tell her I was the one made you come too far, and we were having so much fun we forgot the time. That's the truth."

"But it's no kind of excuse my mama will listen to," May sighed. "I just better get ready for a lickin'."

"One thing for sure," she said a little later, "don't you dare mention Mr. King. Did Mama know he was in the woods, she'd lock me in the house and throw the key away!"

"But he's a nice person!" I protested. "You know that!"

"Rosalee," she said gently, "you know how mamas are."

Bud met us at the edge of the woods. I could tell by the look on his face that he was tempted to say "I told you so!" but he didn't. He ignored me.

"You better hurry!" he said to May. "Mama's mad enough to chomp through a board."

May turned and looked at me. "Maybe you better go on home."

78

I shook my head. My feet were inclined to follow her advice, but my conscience was not. "If you're in trouble, it's my fault. The least I can do is tell your mama, even if she won't think it's a good excuse."

Mrs. Thomas was standing on the back porch when we came into the yard. She looked tired and angry. I was reminded of Mom.

"Let Bud take the pony to the barn," she said, not smiling. May got down without a word and Bud led Baby Doll away. I know he wanted to stay and hear us get what-for, but he had to mind his mama.

"I did the ironing," she went on.

May stood on one foot, then on the other, and looked down at the ground.

"It was my fault," I said. "We were having such a good time, we—"

"May knows what she has to do!"

I found myself looking down at the ground, too, feeling littler and more ashamed than ever in my life. A chicken walked by and scratched at the dirt near my feet. I wished I was home.

"Y'all wash your hands at the pump. I'll bring your lunch out here to the porch." The screen door slammed. I raised my head and caught May's eye.

"I got to go home," I whispered.

"She fixed for us both," May whispered back. Mrs. Thomas came out again pushing the door open with her arm as she carried two plates in her large hands.

"Hurry and wash so you can eat this before the flies gets it," she ordered. May worked the rusty pump handle up and down a few times until the water gushed out. She pumped for me and I pumped for her. Mrs. Thomas handed us our plates without a word.

"Thank you," I said.

"Mmmmhmmm," she said, going back to the kitchen. Shortly she returned with two glasses of cold buttermilk.

Our lunch was leftover cornbread, cold roast pork, and homemade peach pie. Riding ponies and sitting for portraits can certainly make a person ravenous. I ate everything on my plate and licked my fingers.

Mrs. Thomas came to the door again. "You want some more?"

"No, ma'am, thank you," I said and got to my feet. I held out the empty plate and glass. "It was delicious. You sure can cook."

She almost smiled. "Glad you enjoyed it," she said and took our dishes.

"We'll wash the dishes," I volunteered.

"No," she answered.

"I wish I knew a way to make it up to her," I whispered to May when Mrs. Thomas had gone back to the kitchen again.

May shrugged. "I don't know what it'd be. I just wish she'd go ahead and give me a lickin' and get it over with instead of waitin' to tell Pa. Waitin' for judgment gets me down!"

I did not like the thought of May getting punished, especially when it was my fault. In desperation I said, "I do not intend to leave until I do something useful that'll put your mama in a better frame of mind."

May folded her arms and looked out across the grass-bare yard, shaking her head. "The only thing I know of is the garden—the weeds need choppin', but the middle of the day is no time—"

I jumped off the porch. "Get me a hoe!"

"I b'lieve I'd nearly rather take a lickin'," May mur-

mured, but she came along with me. We got a couple of hoes out of the shed and set to work under the broiling sun. It was hot, hard work, but we went at it with conviction. A long time later Ed came out to the garden with two glasses of iced tea.

"Mama says y'all to go sit in the shade and drink this," he said, squinting up at us.

"I'm 'fraid if I sit in the shade I'll never be able to get up again," May groaned, straightening her back.

"Rosalee right red in the face," Ed observed. "She'll pass out if y'all don't rest."

My heart was pounding sort of hard, but the drink gave me a new lease on life, and we finished the last two rows in no time. What I craved to do most at that point was to lie down in the shade of a tree and take a long nap, but it was near three o'clock and I knew Mom would wonder where I was.

"Wait a minute," May said when we had put the hoes away, "I'll get Bud's bike and ride partway with you."

"You'd better ask your mama."

"She's laying down for a nap," May said as she danced away. "She won't care."

I walked down to the road. In a minute May came wheeling around to the front yard on a shiny, new boy's bike. It was bright green and chrome, with a basket, a headlight, and not a single rusty spot. I eyed it with envy. Mine had looked that good, once.

"Are you sure Bud won't care if you ride that?"

She tossed her head. "As many times as he rides Baby Doll, he better not care."

It was the singing that got us in trouble. We started singing the songs we had learned in school chorus and the next thing I noticed, we were in sight of my house. The two miles were a lot shorter than they had been in the morning.

"Wow!" May said, starting to turn around. "I didn't have any idea of comin' this far. So long."

"Wait! It's two miles to your house," I said. "At least come get something to drink before you start back. A few more minutes won't matter."

She looked up at the sun. Beads of sweat shone on her forehead. "O.K.," she said at last. "I guess I can do that."

Mom and Timmy were in the front yard. Mom lay in the lounge chair in the sun. She was wearing her pink bathing suit and had a damp towel wrapped around her head and face to keep from getting overheated. I could not tell if she was asleep or not, but she did not give any signs of hearing Timmy's fretfulness. His playpen was in the shade, but he was bored. When he caught sight of us, he outdid himself smiling and jabbering. I must admit that when Timmy smiles, you would just about lay your heart at his feet if you didn't know better, which I do. But May was taken in. As soon as we leaned the bikes against the fence, she went through the gate straight to the playpen, and knelt beside it.

"Heyo, there, little boy!" she whispered.

Timmy showed his eight teeth and poked her brown cheek with one wet finger.

"I just love babies, don't you?" she sighed.

"They're all right, I guess," I shrugged. "But they sure are constant."

"We probably won't have any more babies at our house," May said. She sounded regretful.

"You can have Timmy if you want him. I'll trade you him for Baby Doll."

We both laughed, and Timmy joined in even though he didn't get the joke. Deep down we knew neither of us would trade. Sometimes the things that are the most trouble are the ones you love most.

Our noise roused Mom. She sat up and unwound the towel from around her eyes and head, like some kind of Egyptian mummy rising from a three-thousand-year sleep. It took a while for her eyes to get used to the sun. Her face was almost as pink as her bathing suit. I thought she looked kind of cute, for an older lady.

"Well, you're back," she said to me. "Where've you been?" Her gaze fell on May. "Oh. Hello."

May stood tall and put both hands behind her. "Hello."

"May was riding partway home with me and before we knew it we were here!" I explained. I wondered why I was talking so loud. "We're going to get some Kool-Aid."

"Oh," said Mom. She didn't seem to know what to say next. She started wrapping the towel around her head again. "Well. You two had better stay outside in the backyard. Don't mess up the house—I've cleaned it for the weekend."

"We're just going to get something to drink!" I said, feeling about as mortified as the day when Bill Steed insulted Mr. King. What did she think we were going to do, for goodness' sake—crayon the walls? I decided Mom and I were going to have to have a heart-to-heart talk about manners. Grown-ups have their failings in that respect too.

As we started into the house, Timmy began to howl.

May gave him a longing look. "Couldn't I just pick him up and hold him?"

"If you want to," I said. I cannot imagine why anyone would want to hold him if they did not have to, but May was tickled to death. So was Timmy. We took him inside with us and shared our grape Kool-Aid with him. He liked that, of course, although he was not aware of the magnitude of the crime when he spilled his on the floor Mom had just waxed! May held him while I wiped up the mess.

I had just washed and wrung out the wiping rag and hung it to dry when Mom burst into the kitchen. The damp towel was draped around her neck, and she looked extremely annoyed.

"Someone wants you out front," she said to May.

May's eyes got wide, and then afraid. Silently she handed Timmy over to me and went out the kitchen and through the hall. I followed as fast as I could with Timmy balanced on one hip.

An old Ford sat in the road in front of our gate with the engine still running. May's pa was at the wheel, and Bud was getting out of the front seat.

"Get in here!" Mr. Thomas snapped at May. Without a word she slid into the seat beside him. She looked ready to faint.

"Wh—what about Bud's bike?" I stammered.

May's hand went to her mouth. Bud glared. "Did you ride my bike up here without askin' me?"

"I sure did!" May said with some of her old spunk. "You ride Baby Doll without—"

"Hush up!" roared Mr. Thomas.

It was like somebody had closed down the lid of a box on them.

"Bud, you ride the bike home," his pa ordered.

"Aw, Pa—she brought it here. Why don't you make her do it?"

"Do what I say. This girl's goin' home right now and take what's comin' to her!" Mr. Thomas shifted the gears roughly and gave me an angry look.

When Bud saw his precious bike leaned so carelessly against our fence, he was more furious than ever. He stood there muttering while his pa turned the car around in our driveway and eased forward into the road. At that moment a long, red car with a foxtail on the radio antenna came barreling along at about sixty miles an hour, which is too fast for anything to travel on Widows Row. Mr. Thomas had to swerve to keep from being rammed in the side. The red car's brakes squealed and the tires skidded, and through the rising dust and exhaust I saw Bill Steed. His mouth moved. From the expression on his face I am sure that what he was saying was not exactly poetry.

He looked hard at Bud and me, sneered at Mr. Thomas, gunned his unmuffled engine, and roared off, leaving the two of us to choke on his dirt.

"I hope you're satisfied!" Bud said to me. He jerked his bike around by its shiny chrome handlebars, threw a leg over the crossbar, and raced away down the road behind his pa's Ford. I thought he must be pretty strong after all, to make the bike go that fast in such squishy dirt.

9

✿✿✿✿✿✿✿✿✿✿✿

Sunday school classrooms at Mt. Carmel Methodist Church are small white boxes situated on a hall at the rear of the building. Being first to arrive at our class the next morning, I took a seat in one of the folding metal chairs and looked out of the square-paned window at the graveyard. The graveyard is a peaceful, quiet place, where daily strife is forgotten and the occupants have learned that all is Vanity.

I am not exactly sure whether all is Vanity, but I can certainly see how a person would come to believe it. All night I had been wondering what May was having to endure. The bad part was, I couldn't even go to her house and ask about her without making things worse. My own Mom and Daddy had hardly spoken a word to me since the previous afternoon, except for stuff like "Pass the biscuits," or "Go take your bath."

Mrs. Hadley, who teaches the girls' class, came clonking in. She nodded at me and sat down in the main chair at the front of the room. She riffled through the Bible and the Sunday school literature and said, "Did you study the lesson about the good Samaritan, Rosalee?"

I looked down at my hands. "No, ma'am. I have been busy."

"So I understand," she said. I did not have time to ask what she meant by that, as Bonnie Lewis chose that moment to come in.

"Hey, there, Rosalee," she said.

"Hey." I looked out at the graveyard.

"I hear you're making *lots* of money working for Jenny Chapman," she went on. She flounced herself to the chair nearest Mrs. Hadley and sat down. Mrs. Hadley leaned forward so as to get the full benefit of my reply.

"I don't know where you heard that," I said.

I had never heard anything so silly in all my days. It is very hard for me to keep my mouth shut sometimes, but I did it that day, as I knew anything I might say would only be more grist for Bonnie's mill. Fortunately, all the other girls came streaming in at that moment, and the conversation came to an end. By the time they were seated, nine girls were clumped together on one side of the room and I was by myself on the other.

"Rosalee," Mrs. Hadley said, "wouldn't you like to come over and sit with the rest of the girls?"

Their sideways looks and giggles were not lost on me.

"I guess not," I said, looking out at the graveyard again.

When I went outside after Sunday school to meet Mom and Daddy, I was somewhat surprised to see them standing off to themselves. That is most unusual, particularly for Daddy, as he has always been the main man in any conversational group in the churchyard. When I was little, I could stand behind his legs and hear a good bit of the talk among the men, but they notice me now and won't talk while I am around. It is one of the sadnesses of growing up.

Daddy's white Sunday shirt was damp with sweat and his tie seemed too tight, but he looked very handsome. He never wears a coat to church in summer. None of the men do, except the Reverend Filbert, and I guess that is because he came to Arnold's Corners from the outside world. Mom's peach-colored dress made her look young. I was proud of them both. I skipped across the churchyard in and out among people and arrived somewhat breathless beside Mom and Daddy. I accidentally stumbled against Daddy.

"Rosalee, for goodness' sakes try to act your age! You're making a spectacle of yourself!" Mom scolded, looking around to see if anybody had noticed. She could have saved herself the trouble, as nobody in Arnold's Corners ever misses anything in the nature of a spectacle.

"What are you doing over here by yourselves?" I asked.

Mom gave me a pained look. "*You* ought to know!"

Well, I did not know, but I had sense enough to know that she would think I was being sassy if I said so. I changed the subject.

"Are we going to preaching?"

"Don't we usually go to preaching?" Daddy said.

It is hard to deal with parents who are acting thus. I decided to stay out of their way until they were in a better mood.

"We're going in the church in about ten minutes!" Daddy said as I started away. "Don't go far."

As it turned out, I did not have to go far. I got an earful right away. Mrs. Crifton, who is on the heavy side, was telling Bonnie Lewis' mother and Toobie Wells about a horrifying experience she had recently undergone. I bent down and buckled my sandal and listened.

"—he stopped that funny ve-hickel right in front of my house last Tuesday morning. Honestly I was scared to death! See, I wasn't even dressed yet—still in my housecoat—and I heard this noise of a car, and I peeped out between the curtains because I thought maybe Doreen—my daughter—had decided to come by early, and *there he was!* Well, you can just imagine how I *felt!* All that hair—why, shivers just run up and down my back!"

I thought about that for a minute. Mrs. Crifton with the shivers would probably be something to behold!

"He got out of that—that thing and stood beside it looking right at my house. I purely had the feeling he could see me through the walls! Honestly, I didn't even have the strength to go lock the front door!"

"What did he *do?*" Toobie wanted to know.

"Nothing, as it turned out," Mrs. Crifton said. She sounded disappointed. "Except to pace up and down and stare at my house and talk to himself. I could see his lips moving!" She put a hand on her heaving bosom. "I think he's dangerous! People like that ought to be locked up . . ."

The ladies nodded. I myself was astounded, for it had finally dawned on me that Mrs. Crifton was talking about Mr. King. Was she making up the whole thing? I could not picture him going through all those gyrations in front of her house, although she does live in a kind of oddity built of stucco and painted pink with aqua trim.

It is the only house of its kind in Berry County. It is not beautiful by any stretch of the imagination, however, and I could not credit Mr. King, with all the places he has been, showing that much interest in it.

I was getting a cramp in my leg from kneeling, so I stood up, but did not walk away.

"I know what you mean," Mrs. Lewis was saying. "No *normal* person would act the way he does. Why, I heard the other day that somebody had seen him up on that ridge overlooking Ivy Holloman's farm, and that he had some kind of drawing board and was making marks and talking to himself—just like you say."

"—and Papa says he's come into Hooker's several times lately," Toobie Wells chimed in. "He gets his mail and then stands around to listen. Papa says it's got so they all just hush when he comes in—they won't even talk till he leaves."

"That ought to get to him after a while," Mrs. Crifton allowed. "A person ought to be able to tell where he's not welcome."

"I don't know," said Toobie. "Papa claims he has this funny way of staring at people. Says he looks at you like he's memorizing your features or something. Don't that sound like a spy to you?"

"Well, I'm sure Hooker would be just as glad if he never came back," Mrs. Lewis said. "He ought to do his trading at Brigham's, after what happened between him and Bill Steed the other day. That daughter of Tal's . . . Do you know she and my Bonnie were actually best friends once? Honestly, that girl has just gone *wild*. You ought to hear what Bill saw over at Tal and Elizabeth's house yesterday afternoon!"

She darted a look around and caught sight of me standing there. I was feeling slightly sick and I guess my face showed it. She pursed her lips, drew herself up, and turned her back on me. The three ladies whispered together and went into the church for preaching. I was glad they had seen me.

I could have defended Mr. King's actions on the ridge overlooking Ivy Holloman's. I could have told those ladies that he was probably doing a sketch of the farm for fun, but what good would that have done? People in Arnold's Corners would think him all the crazier for spending his time in the good working part of the day drawing pictures. They would probably say he was a spy, too, without taking into account that there is nothing in all of Arnold's Corners that even *I* would want to spy upon! And as for what Bill Steed had seen at our house the day before, he couldn't have seen anything in those few seconds but Bud and Mr. Thomas and May, and he has seen them lots of times.

About the only thing I noticed as we were leaving after the service was that the congregation gave us Brighams a wide berth. I am used to it, of course, being the kind of person I am, but Mom and Daddy, being more usual and respected in the community, were not.

Timmy and I occupied the back seat on the way home. He was tired and fussy and snuggled close to me. I looked out of the window at the fields and houses.

"I am sick and tired of this place!" I said aloud, although I was really talking to myself.

"Well," said Mom unexpectedly, "it's your own fault if you are!"

"What do you mean?" I said.

"It's these people you take up with," she said. "Arnold's Corners is full of ordinary, respectable men, women, and children. But you choose to spend your time with a colored girl, a hippie from who knows where, and a strange woman with a baby and no husband. I do not know how to spell it out any plainer than that. You seem bound and determined to make a curiosity of yourself—and the rest of us, as far as that goes. You don't seem to care one bit what your behavior does to your father's business or to our standing in the community!"

I do not know whether you have ever been so angry you could not speak. Arguing is no good at a time like that because when you argue you have to have some reasonable hope that you can persuade the other person to see your point of view. And even I had sense enough to realize that in this case it was out of the question.

I did not agree with Mom. I could not see how the people I associated with would affect Daddy's business. In my opinion, his problem was from not filling up the front post office corner and in not honoring gasoline credit cards, but I didn't say so.

10

❁❁❁❁❁❁❁❁❁❁❁

You can't help the way you feel about people. If you like them, you want to be with them. If you don't, it is wise to stay out of their way as much as possible. This has always been my philosophy. But now my own Mom and Daddy were telling me that I had no business liking the three most interesting, likable people in my life. And that, furthermore, my whole family would suffer for it if I persisted.

Such a thing puts a person on the spot where loyalties are concerned. You ask yourself, Who is right? The logical answer is your parents, because they have lived longer and are more experienced. But what if your insides will not let you believe that? It is a headachy question. I began to have a better idea of what Mr. King meant by Double Vision.

By nine thirty Monday morning my chores were all done. Mom seemed to be waiting for me to say something, but I will not make promises that I don't think I can keep. It is not honorable. I wondered if she expected me to quit my job. She did not say it, however, so I left as usual.

I stepped out into the drizzle under Mom's big old umbrella. I let its steel ribs rest directly on top of my copper highlights so nobody passing would see my face. I figured that traveling unrecognized was the least I could do for my family, under the circumstances. However, walking along in this manner made it difficult to see where I was going.

"I beg your pardon," said a deep voice almost at my elbow. "Could you tell me—"

I must have jumped a foot. I lifted the umbrella and peered out. There was Mr. King in his painty denims with a big flat plastic-covered rectangle under his arm. From the size, I judged it was his sketch pad. I do not know which of us was the more astounded, but he was first to recover.

"You are everywhere, Lady Rose!"

I shook my head. "No, I am hardly anywhere at all these days. *You* are the one who is everywhere, as I understand it."

He gave me a cautious look. "Oh?"

"Yes," I said. "I may as well tell you for your own good, you are attracting considerable attention." I heard the hum of a car up the road and put the umbrella way down over my head again. I resumed walking, with him in step beside me. The vehicle passed us by.

"I take it you mean unfavorable attention," he said, after a short silence.

"Yes," I said. "As I have explained to you before, in Arnold's Corners if people don't know every single fact, they make up some on the strength of what they think they see."

"And what do they think they see?"

I was ashamed. It was a burden for me to have to tell him. I was glad to have the umbrella to hide under.

"They *think* they see a—a hippie, whatever that is. Or a . . . crazy man who talks to himself and makes marks on big paper tablets. Or a spy. Or a dangerous criminal who goes around memorizing people's faces so he can attack them at a defenseless moment."

Mr. King began to laugh. I lifted the umbrella again so I could see his face.

"You do not see the seriousness of this!" I said severely. He quit laughing then, but his eyes were merry.

"I'm sorry," he apologized. "It's so incredible. My intentions toward Arnold's Corners have been nothing but honorable, believe me."

"I believe you," I said, "but you may as well know that I am about the only one who does."

He did not seem very perturbed. "I'm sorry that people don't want me around, but I'm really not surprised."

I pressed my lips together. Why would a person insist on staying where he wasn't welcome? "It's no fun, not being wanted," I said. "I *know!*"

"But you stay," he said.

"Only because I'm not of age—it wouldn't do me any good to run away—the law could drag me back."

"But," he said, "what if you knew you could leave—that you could get away scot-free and nobody would try to stop you."

I opened my mouth to say that of course I'd leave in a flash, but I closed it again.

"Poor Lady Rose," he said. "I am sorry if you have gotten into trouble because of me."

I wondered how he knew, then decided he probably knew everything, being part Indian and also unusually

95

wise for a grown-up. "If I am in trouble," I said, lifting my chin, "it is nobody's fault but my own."

The sky had been getting darker, but I was so wrapped up in the conversation that I didn't take proper note. All of a sudden the pattering on top of my umbrella became a roar. The rain came down in sheets.

"You'll drown!" I shouted, breaking into a run. "That's Jenny Chapman's house over there, where I baby-sit. Run for the porch!"

I did not stop to see whether he was taking my advice, as it is exceedingly hard to run in windy rain with an oversized umbrella. By the time the two of us reached the cover of Jenny's front porch, Mr. King was in a saturated condition. Water streamed from the ends of his mustache and from his shirt sleeves. Even his shoes squished when he took a step.

"Well," he said, holding his arms out to each side to drip, "it's a good thing I wrapped the sketch pad in plastic—otherwise a whole summer's work would have gone down the drain."

I started to ask him if he didn't mean, instead, a whole summer's fun, but Jenny came to the door just then.

"Heavens! You're soaked!" she gasped.

"Well," I said, "as you can see, I am not nearly so waterlogged as Mr. King here. Mr. King, this is Jenny Chapman."

He nodded wetly. "How do you do?" Little drops of water made tracks down the side of his face.

Jenny didn't seem to know what to say. I keep forgetting that grown-ups have different rules from kids. I suppose she was trying to figure how she could politely let me inside without inviting him in too.

"Mr. King is staying in Arnold's Corners," I explained. "He is a friend of mine."

"Oh," Jenny said. "Well—uh—won't you come in until the shower is over?"

Mr. King seemed very embarrassed, which is a side of him I had not seen but once. "I couldn't do that," he said. "I'll drip all over your floors—"

"Nothing could happen to these floors that hasn't already happened to them," Jenny said with conviction.

I left my umbrella open on the porch and wiped my wet feet on the welcome mat. Mr. King and his plastic parcel waited until Jenny got towels to catch some of the water while I went into the front room to clear material and dresses off the extra chair so he would have a place to sit. Ruthie started yelling at the top of her lungs. She has discovered the full capacity of her vocal cords and rejoices in using them. I lifted her out of the playpen and set her on the floor.

"I feel badly about this," Mr. King said as he came in with Jenny. "Don't feel that you have to interrupt your work and entertain me."

"A few minutes won't matter," Jenny said. "I'll catch up."

She excused herself to make some coffee. It was left to Ruthie and me to do the entertaining. Ruthie was amazed. She is not used to seeing men, as all of Jenny's customers are ladies—or at least women. She leaned way back to see his face and fell over backward with a thump.

Before I could move, Mr. King was down on his knees beside her. He helped her sit up again, then moved away a little. She looked from him to me, trying to decide by our faces whether to cry. I kept my face as blank as I could, because I have heard Ruthie cry and do not like to encourage that kind of noise.

Mr. King took something out of his pocket. It was about the size of a baby's fist—red and blue plastic twisted into a funny shape. He laid it on the palm of his hand and held it out for Ruthie's inspection. She studied the shape carefully and then looked at him. I tried to imagine any of the men I knew kneeling on the floor like that, smiling and gentle. It taxed my imagination.

Finally, she reached out and took the object. I held my breath while she turned it around in her hand, felt it, and at last bit it. That decided the matter. She gave Mr. King an enormous smile.

By the time Jenny came back with the coffeepot and cups, Ruthie was sitting on Mr. King's lap chewing the plastic object. I felt useless, as without Ruthie to chase there was not much for me to do.

"Oh, my," Jenny said. "How did she manage that?"

"She smiled and I was lost." He laughed. "But the toy helped. I've been working on that design for some time, but this is its first true test."

Jenny's eyes brightened. "Do you like to design things?"

He nodded. "As a sort of sideline."

"That's what I always wanted to do," Jenny said as she poured coffee into three cups. Her long hair fell forward so that I could not see her face as she talked, but I could hear the sadness in her voice. "When I was Rosalee's age my great ambition was to design elegant ball gowns for very rich ladies. I used to drape myself with Mother's window curtains!"

"And what is your ambition now?" he asked quietly.

"To eat!" She handed me one of the cups of coffee. I was taken aback, not only by her answer, but also by the fact that she offered me coffee. I do not ever drink the stuff, but when someone is nice enough to treat you like a person, you should not complain about the refreshments. I had learned more about Jenny in the few minutes since Mr. King came to her house than in all the time I had known her. He is like that—you find yourself telling stuff you'd never breathe to any regular person. Maybe it is because he is not trying to find out things from curiosity, but because he really cares about people.

"Mr. King is a pretty good drawer," I said, to contribute something to the conversation. "If he has the picture he drew of May and me, maybe he would show it to you . . ."

"All right—I'll do that," he said. He finished his coffee in about three gulps, set Ruthie on the floor by his chair, and removed the damp plastic from the sketch pad. As he turned the pages, I saw what he meant by a whole summer's work.

Besides the sketch of May and me on the rock, there was Mrs. Crifton's house, which I recognized at once even without the pink and aqua. I could almost see her in her housecoat peering out through the curtains. I recognized Miss Ivy Holloman's farm from having been up on the ridge myself on summer days. Our store was there, so plain you felt you could walk right into the picture and buy an orange pushup. And Hooker's, too —all it lacked was a few flies, but I guess that would have been pushing things too far.

I did not know what to say. The whole of Arnold's Corners was laid out on those pages. The very last page was full of faces, some sketched in, some still in outline. I recognized Mr. Purdy Brown, Les Barton, Mr. Hooker, Bill Steed, and even my own daddy!

"How splendid!" Jenny said, looking at the picture of May and me. "You've gotten everybody."

"Not entirely," he smiled. He put the plastic covering on again. "I'd like to do a drawing of you and Ruthie too, along with the others. Could I come back sometime? Perhaps in the evening when you've finished sewing—"

"We don't belong to Arnold's Corners," she said, looking away.

"I think you do," he said.

I finally got my voice back. "Mr. King, you are too talented to waste your life! You are going to have to quit painting walls and go to drawing full time."

"What?" Jenny was puzzled. "Painting walls?"

"Well—" he began.

"Never mind," she said, with a one-sided smile. She pointed toward the piles of half-finished garments scattered around the room. "I know a person has to eat. What I do is certainly a long way from designing elegant ball gowns."

"Maybe not such a long way at all," he said seriously. "A little salesmanship might create a market—"

"For ball gowns in Arnold's Corners?" Jenny laughed.

"Well," he said, "maybe not for ball gowns, but for well-designed custom-made clothes. Arnold's Corners women spend money for clothes. It's just a matter of introducing them to real quality."

Jenny was not convinced. "They'd never pay the prices. I'd be out of work in a week."

Mr. King looked as though he wanted to say something else, but thought better of it. Instead he looked at his watch and then out the window.

"The rain has almost stopped," he said as he stood

up. He tucked the sketch pad under his left arm again and shook hands with Jenny. "Thanks for the coffee—I hope I didn't take up too much of your working time."

Jenny's cheeks got rosy, which is very obvious on such a pale person. "I'm glad you came. Here—don't forget your toy!" She knelt beside Ruthie. "O.K., Baby, let Mr. King have the toy."

Ruthie had other ideas. She let forth a yell that made me want to stick my fingers in my ears.

"Let her keep it," he chuckled. "She has earned it."

As Jenny went with him to the door I heard him ask again whether she would be willing to sit for him. I did not hear her answer. I picked up Ruthie and watched through the bay window as he trudged off down the road.

"I hope you aren't mad at me for bringing a perfect stranger in unannounced like that," I said when Jenny came back. "He was so wet! You don't have to pay me for the time he was here."

"Don't be ridiculous!" Jenny exclaimed as she sat down at the sewing machine. "It was a nice break. I should pay you double." She began to sew. I could hear her humming above the buzz of the electric motor. I could not ever remember hearing her hum before. It is amazing what a little bit of company can do for a person's spirits on a rainy day!

11

❁❁❁❁❁❁❁❁❁❁❁❁❁

I was relieved to see Peter York Hopper at the store when I arrived that afternoon. Peter York is a cheerful person and a cut above the types that hang around on rainy days. He is the route salesman for the R. D. Drug Company. He supplies us with such necessaries as mineral oil, liniment, tooth powder, hair restorer, and denture cleaner, which have always been big sellers at Daddy's store. I like Peter York because he respects a girl's intelligence if she happens to have some, which I have always felt I did. Also, he does not call me "Red."

He had his book and was taking down Daddy's order.

"Now—we have a new item," he told Daddy. "Something that's been in demand for a long while, but R. D. took the time to manufacture a *quality* product."

Daddy leaned forward trying to see into Peter York's big black sample case. Peter York sneaked a hand under the flap and brought out a straight up-and-down bottle of clear red stuff.

102

"This is R. D. Effervescent Mouthwash, good as anything on the market—and much less expensive. Any dentist will tell you that R. D.'s Effervescent works as well as any of the other mouthwashes that cost more. And it tastes just *great!*" He unscrewed the top and offered Daddy a fleeting sniff. "Why, you have to be careful when you take a mouthful to swish it around and spit it out—it tastes so good you almost want to drink it."

Daddy regarded the bottle. "I don't know, Peter York. Business has been mighty slow—"

Peter York coughed behind his hand and looked down at the floor. Obviously he had been hearing something about Daddy's troubles.

"I don't know if I can even sell the usual stuff," Daddy went on, "much less this."

"Why not let me set up a special display?" Peter York suggested. "Right up there in the front of the store where the post office used to be? That big window—"

"Nope." Daddy turned his mouth down and shook his head. "I'm not putting anything in that front corner."

"But the display will only be so big," Peter York persisted, showing how big with his spread-out arms.

"No," said Daddy. "Give me six bottles of the red stuff and I'll see what it does."

Peter York was disappointed, but Daddy has always been a good customer, so he did not argue. When they were done transacting and Peter York was ready to go, he said to me, "Rosalee, my buggy's out of gas. How much would you charge to fill 'er up?"

"I don't charge, except for the gas." I grinned. He followed me out front, where his station wagon was

103

parked near the pump. The whole back was filled with boxes and cases.

"What's all that stuff?" I asked, taking down the hose and turning the indicator to a row of zeros.

"Samples. A salesman always has to carry samples with him—people like to see what they're getting."

My brain began to click and hum right along with the gas pump. I recalled what Mr. King had said that morning, about how a little salesmanship might create a market for Jenny's special talent.

"Tell me about selling," I said.

Peter York gave me an odd look. "What do you want to know?"

"Anything you've got to tell," I said.

So while the tank was filling, I got a short course in salesmanship.

"The first thing," said Peter York, "is that you have to be sincere." He fixed an earnest expression upon me, so I could see what he meant. It involved a little bit of a frown, narrowed eyes, and a slight leaning forward. I thought probably I could do that, with practice.

"It also helps if you can have an eye-catching display where people will see it," he added regretfully, casting a look back at the store. "But in any case, you have to make your prospect feel that he can't do without your product. Now—that is not easy, because he has been doing without it all these months and years.

"Say it is somebody you've never done business with before," he continued. "Make friends—get on his side, so to speak. I try to find out what such a prospect is interested in. What're his politics. How many people in his family. What kind of car he drives. This is called The Warmup. The point is to find out what we have in common. Then, when I feel we're on a one-to-one, I in-

104

troduce him to my line by showing him items I think his customers will be most likely to use."

"Like mineral oil?" I offered.

"Exactly. Of course, the main rule to start with is: Never Work for a Company That Doesn't Believe in Quality. Otherwise, you'll have all the customers on your back, and you'll end up with the responsibility of returning their money." He struck a pose. "If you're going to live where you sell, you have to be able to hold up your head when you meet your customers and friends. You can't give them anything shoddy."

"I see," I said. "But I still don't understand how you make a person feel he can't do without your product another minute when he has been doing without it all along."

Peter York looked at me a moment, then paid for the gas and got into the station wagon. "Do you know something, Rosalee? The truth is, I don't know either. I do it all the time, and I can't for the life of me pick it apart and tell you how."

"Well," I said, as he started the engine, "you do a good job. I am still thirsty for a drink of R. D.'s Effervescent Mouthwash."

Peter York hollered with laughter as he drove away.

It does a person good to see someone so cheerful, especially when you don't have anything to be cheerful about yourself.

Tuesday morning began a lot the same as Monday, except it was sunny and hot. I rode the bike to Jenny's because muddy roads make good exercise, and exercise helps to take your mind off your troubles.

Jenny was out on her porch holding Ruthie on one arm and her pocketbook under the other.

"Good! I'm glad you have the bike," she said.

"Would you take this dollar to your dad's store and see if he might have a seven-inch red zipper?"

"Sure." I rode up to the porch and reached for the dollar. Then I had a better idea. "But why don't I stay with Ruthie while you go? You can ride my bike."

"Oh, I don't know whether I even remember how to ride one," she said, looking doubtful.

"Yes, you do. Riding a bicycle is like breathing—once you learn how, you don't ever forget till you die." I jumped off. "Go ahead—it'll be fun for you."

For a second I thought she was going to say no, but finally she sort of shrugged and said, "O.K., I will."

I watched her pedaling away. Bent over the handlebars, with her hair streaming out behind, she looked very young. Ruthie began to whimper, and I sat down on the top step to play with her. That is the main reason why I didn't see Mrs. Crifton until she was at the bottom step and on her way up.

"Howdy, Rosalee," she puffed, plodding up the steps. "You having troubles?"

"No, ma'am," I said. "Just trying to keep Ruthie happy till Jenny gets back."

Mrs. Crifton reached the porch and stood there a moment gasping for breath. "She going to be gone long?"

"No, ma'am. She just went to the store for a zipper."

Mrs. Crifton took my answer as an invitation to stay and sat down in the porch rocker. "I been seeing you come over here every day," she said.

"Yes, ma'am. I tend to Ruthie while Jenny sews."

"Does she pay you good?"

I vow I have lived in Arnold's Corners all my life, but I still can't get used to the point-blank way people ask questions that are none of their business. "She pays me as well as she can, under the circumstances," I said in my cool business voice.

"Oh? Are the—uh—circumstances not so good, then?"

"I merely refer to the fact that *some* people are never willing to pay a fair amount for quality work," I said. "Jenny pays me more than my services are worth, but she is not paid anything like what hers are!"

Mrs. Crifton's lips tightened. "I came," she announced, "to see if Jenny'd make me a dress for Doreen's wedding week after next. I already picked out the material. It's going to be a formal occasion—eight o'clock wedding—so I need to have a long dress. I thought Jenny could make something pretty for not too much—say four dollars or so."

I had to bite my tongue. A good salesman, I reminded myself, gets on the good side of the customer. "Actually," I said, setting Ruthie on the porch beside me, "Jenny charges at least ten dollars for a formal."

I could not believe I had said it, but I had.

Mrs. Crifton's little green eyes glazed over. "What's that? Why, Rosalee, you know you made that up!"

"Mrs. Crifton," I said, leaning forward and lowering my voice, "Jenny Chapman is no ordinary, run-of-the-mill seamstress. People in Arnold's Corners are not aware that she is a talented designer. Someday the name of J. Chapman is going to appear on dress labels. Quality is not cheap!"

"I never said it was!" Mrs. Crifton responded. She might have gotten up and stonked off then and there, but it was too much of an effort.

I was feeling nervous. I, more than anybody, know full well that it does not take any kind of urging at all to get a rumor off and running in Arnold's Corners. But

Jenny *was* a talented designer—I had seen what her talent could do for shapeless ladies. I turned my full, earnest attention upon Mrs. Crifton.

"Bring your material over," I said. "Tell Jenny you want an exclusive outfit like nobody in Berry County has ever seen before. And say, 'Spare no expense!'" I flung an arm outward to emphasize the words. "Wouldn't it be worth more than ten dollars to you to have the only different-looking dress at your daughter's wedding?"

"Well, I certainly wouldn't want to outshine the bride," Mrs. Crifton hedged, but the battle was going on within. "I'll think about it.

"You tell Jenny I'll be back," Mrs. Crifton said as she heaved herself off the rocking chair and started down the porch steps. "I don't know if I want to pay that much or not."

"You would never regret it," I said, more earnest than ever. "One of the few pleasures a woman has in life is knowing she is tastefully dressed in distinctive clothes. Don't you think so?"

"Well, yes, I guess so. I'll be back."

Fortunately, she was concentrating so hard on the steps that she did not see Jenny coming along the road on the bicycle. By the time Jenny rode into the yard, Mrs. Crifton was safely beyond the hedge and on her way home. I was relieved.

"What did she want?" Jenny asked, jumping off the bike.

"Mrs. Crifton is willing to pay ten dollars or more for a long dress for Doreen's wedding," I announced carefully. "On the condition that it be different from everybody else's."

Jenny stared. "Did she say that?"

108

"More or less," I allowed. "She'll be back—she said."

Jenny started up the steps, shaking her head in disbelief. "Miracles will never cease!"

Well, that depends upon your understanding of what a miracle is. I, for one, am of a more practical nature.

12

❋❋❋❋❋❋❋❋❋❋❋❋

Mrs. Crifton came the very next day, bringing her sky-blue linen material. She did not say a word about the price—just told Jenny she hoped she'd get her money's worth.

By lunchtime on Thursday, Jenny had already cut out the dress, having made the pattern herself. She was excited because it was the first time since she had come to Arnold's Corners that she had ever been free to do what she liked best. She showed me a picture of how the dress was going to look. Of course, in the sketch it was worn by a tall, graceful lady who bore about as much of a resemblance to Mrs. Crifton as I do to the Emperor of Japan. I said so. Jenny laughed and said she could understand my doubts, but then she showed me how, on a plump lady, certain lines have what she calls a "slimming effect." I could see then that the sky-blue linen might turn out to be something after all. At least it might make Mrs. Crifton *feel* like the tall, graceful lady, and that is what really matters, I guess. I stayed a little longer both Thursday and Friday mornings, so she could work.

Friday afternoon Mr. Purdy Brown came to the store in what was, for him, a hurry.

"I guess you heard," he told Daddy as he eased himself down in the chair by the door. "Somebody broke in the feller's trailer or whatever it is and took some of his stuff."

Daddy's eyes narrowed. "What fellow do you mean?"

"You know—that King person Bill Steed spoke so sharp at, here in your store that day," Mr. Purdy said with some impatience.

My heart began to pound.

"Oh," Daddy said. He did not seem inclined to ask any more questions.

"How did you find out about it?" I asked Mr. Purdy, "And what was stolen?"

"They was talkin' about it over to Hooker's yestiddy." Mr. Purdy gave Daddy a sheepish look, not liking to admit being a patron of Hooker's. But I can understand, as what Mr. Purdy dotes on most in this world is companionship, and he certainly could not find very much of it around our place these days.

"I wasn't there at the time," he said, "but they say King came bustin' in about noon yestiddy wanting to know where to contact the law. Said somebody had broke into his camper while he was away and some important stuff had been took."

"But what?" I asked.

"I don't know what it was," said Mr. Purdy.

Why would anybody steal from Mr. King? I tried to remember, from my one time of being inside his camper, what there might be in it that anyone would want to take.

"I hope," I said, "that somebody at Hooker's had the politeness to tell Mr. King how to reach the sheriff."

"I'm surprised he didn't take it up with Lyman," said Mr. Purdy. "Lyman would help him get the sheriff."

"Lyman's been away," Daddy spoke up. That startled me, as I thought he had abandoned the conversation. I wondered how he knew Mr. Lyman had been away. I imagined the scene in Hooker's store, with Mr. King bursting in, desperately seeking help, and all those men just lounging around winking at one another and sort of sneering. I guess I got a bit hysterical.

"I think," said I, "that the good citizens of Arnold's Corners should not condone thievery!"

"Nobody's condoning it, Rosalee," Daddy said.

"What do you call it when a stranger in the community gets robbed and nobody does anything to see that justice is done?"

"Mr. King has not been here to seek my help!" Daddy said.

"Well, then, why not go out and offer it?" I replied. "I would offer mine, except you've as much as forbidden me to pass the time of day with him—"

Daddy threw up his hands. "Girl, you try my patience! I have only just found out about the robbery myself, and here you—I do not know how I put up with you! Why don't you just go home?"

I laid down what I was doing and walked right out the door without so much as a backward look. Our relationship had suffered from the lack of business. Daddy hadn't had much of anybody to talk to lately but me, and I suppose that can get to a person like my daddy, who has always liked people and enjoyed their goodwill. He might have been having failures of confidence too, which is more devastating to a grown-up than it is to somebody like me.

I crossed the highway. It was too early to go home. I did not want to face a long afternoon with Mom and Timmy. What I really wanted was to meet May and Baby Doll somewhere and spend the rest of the day riding and talking—but that was out of the question. I had not seen or heard from May since her pa took her away from our house the previous Saturday. I wondered if her mama had really locked her in. I was thinking these things, and all the time walking along Widows Row, just as though my feet always took me straight home whether I wanted to go there or not.

I stopped in the road in front of Jenny's house. She was sitting at the sewing machine with her back toward the window and did not see me. I went and sat on the bottom step with my elbows on my knees and my chin in my hands. I sat there a long time. I began to have a lumpy feeling somewhere between my chest and chin.

"Why, Rosalee! What are you doing out here in the hot sun?"

I had been so wrapped up in my thoughts that I did not hear Jenny come to the door.

"Hey," I said. It sounded thin. The lumpy feeling made talking hard.

She came down the steps and sat beside me. "Why don't you come inside and get a cold drink?" she said gently. She put an arm around me. I didn't know I was going to cry. Maybe it was because nobody had said anything especially kind to me in several days. I am ashamed to say I bawled. Jenny did not ask me what was wrong the way Mom would have done. I would never cry like that around Mom, because she thinks you have to have an explainable reason for such a thing, which I did not.

"Come on," Jenny said, when I got to the hiccuping stage. "It's too hot here."

I got up and followed her inside. For once in her short life Ruthie was playing quietly in her pen. In her hand was the plastic object Mr. King had given her. That reminded me of his misfortune and I almost started crying again.

"Go to the kitchen and bathe your face with cold water so it won't look red and swollen," Jenny ordered. I obeyed.

"Do you want to tell me about it?" she asked when I came back. She gave me a glass of cold lemonade and sat me down in a chair near the sewing machine.

"I am just feeling generally low," I said. "Probably I need vitamins." But I knew that wasn't so. I found myself telling her about Mr. King's camper being robbed. I did not know if she would even care, having only met him the one time.

"Yes," she said when I had finished, "I knew that."

My mouth dropped open. "You knew it? You mean when I was here this very morning, you knew?"

Jenny nodded. "You remember he asked to sketch Ruthie and me last Monday during his visit. Well—he came the next two evenings after supper, before Ruthie's bedtime. He was supposed to finish last night, but he couldn't."

I was speechless. To think Mr. King had been to Jenny's three times in a row and I hadn't known a thing about it! I have always admired her ability to keep her mouth shut, but this was ridiculous!

"Why couldn't he finish last night?" I asked.

"Because," she answered, "it was his sketch pad that was stolen."

I sat straight up. "His sketch pad? You mean the one with May and me in it? And Mrs. Crifton's house? And . . . and . . ."

"Yes. He was very upset."

"Well, I should guess so!" I jumped to my feet. The enormity of the crime was impossible to believe. "You *know* he said Monday that sketch pad was his whole summer's work! Why would anybody in Arnold's Corners take that? What would they do with it, except maybe tear it up, for meanness?"

"Why does anybody in Arnold's Corners do anything?" Jenny said flatly.

Well, that is exactly the question I have asked all of my thinking life, but I must admit I felt a little funny, hearing Jenny say it.

"Maybe it was a tramp passing through," I said. "Somebody that just happened to stumble across the camper out there in the woods."

Jenny shook her head. Deep down, I did not believe it either. That sketch pad, or one like it, had been in Mr. King's hands practically every time he was seen during the past two weeks. Whoever stole it knew it was important to him.

"Has he been to the sheriff?"

"He was going. I haven't heard today."

"Well," I said, putting my hands in my pockets and looking down at the floor, "I wish you had told me this morning when I was here."

Jenny did not answer at first. Then she said, "I should have. I'm sorry. But I've gotten so used to keeping things to myself . . ."

115

She did not finish the sentence, but she didn't have to.

"It's O.K.," I told her. I guess it is hard for her to trust people too. I thanked her for the lemonade and left.

The first thing Mom asked when I walked into our kitchen was, "What on earth happened to you?"

I did not know what she meant.

"Your eyes look as though you've been crying," she said.

"It wasn't real crying," I said. "A car passed me on the road and I got a face full of dust. Some went in my eyes."

Mom looked at me long and hard but decided not to pursue the subject, for which I was grateful. I do not like to tell extensive fibs.

"You are home early," she said instead.

"Yes. Daddy got tired of me."

"Rosalee, that isn't true. Your daddy dotes on you." Mom's voice was almost kind. I felt my throat getting lumpy again. I tell you, it is not easy for me to handle sympathy. My system is not accustomed to it.

"He has a funny way of showing it," I said.

"He has a lot on his mind these days," she sighed, turning back to the stove. "He's concerned about the business. I'm worried about him, Rosalee. He hardly sleeps at night. That isn't like him."

She was right—Daddy could always sleep after a hard day's work. And it was not like Mom, either, to tell me about it. I felt uneasy. It was almost better to have her scolding and yelling at me.

13

✿✿✿✿✿✿✿✿✿✿✿✿

Mt. Carmel Methodist Church had Homecoming that Sunday. For those who are not familiar with Homecoming it is a special Sunday each year when all the people who ever belonged to a church are invited back for services and a big dinner-on-the-grounds. The main emphasis of the day is on eating. All the women knock themselves out fixing dishes that they are famous for. Mom's specialty is fried chicken, but she also contributes bean salad, a pound cake, a baked ham, and lemon meringue pie. She brings less than some of the women, so you can imagine how much food is on the tables under the trees.

It was a gorgeous, bright day. I was feeling pretty good, in spite of recent circumstances, because lots of elegant food always puts people in high, and sometimes forgiving, spirits.

Timmy sat in the front seat between Mom and Daddy. The food and I were in back. I had my forehead pressed against the window and up ahead I saw a familiar figure walking along the highway, going the same direction as we were. His head was down and his shoulders slumped. I sat up and yelped, "Daddy! There's Mr. King!"

"So I see," Daddy said shortly. Mom leaned forward for a better look. She had heard about Mr. King but had not had the pleasure of meeting him.

"Well, aren't you going to give him a lift?" I asked.

Daddy turned almost full around to look at me. The car veered a little. "You must be out of your mind!" he said. "After what I have been through on account of him, do you think I would pick up that man and take him somewhere of a Sunday morning in my car with my family?" He hunched forward and stepped on the gas pedal. We zoomed past Mr. King, and the breeze we made ruffled his green velvety-looking jacket. I sighed. The day was not so bright anymore.

At Mt. Carmel after preaching the ladies rushed back and forth between the church kitchen and the outdoor tables, putting out their food. Yellow jackets buzzed over the cakes and gelatin salads. The men took off their ties and rolled up their sleeves. Mom and Daddy were right in the middle of things once more. It seemed as though time might take care of some of our problems after all. Maybe, starting Monday morning, business at Brigham's might improve. I helped Mom and the ladies put out the food, and snitched a deviled egg to still the growling in my belly.

All of a sudden a hush fell over the crowd. I bowed my head, expecting the preacher to say grace. I had my eyes squinched, as I was looking directly at the very piece of Mom's chicken that I intended to claim for my plate after the amen.

The Reverend Filbert did not pray. A buzz that was

118

not yellow jackets started at one edge of the crowd and moved in our direction.

". . . It's him!" a lady whispered beside me.

"How could he?" Mrs. Lewis whispered back.

"Who invited *him*, for heaven's sake?" Mrs. Hadley said out loud. I raised my head. Mr. King stood at the edge of the churchyard. He was smiling, but in a more determined way than usual. I did not know what to do, for although my natural inclination was to go to him and make him welcome, I did not wish to make life hard for Mom and Daddy again just when everything was going so well.

Mom put down the dish she was holding and walked around the table straight to Mr. King. She did not look to the right or to the left. I longed for the ground to open and swallow me up, knowing she was going to tell him off.

"Mr. King?" she said in a clear voice when she was in front of him.

"Yes," he said pleasantly, looking down at her.

"I'm Elizabeth Brigham," she said, putting out her right hand to shake his. "Welcome to Mt. Carmel's Homecoming. You're just in time for dinner."

Mom's action put people on the spot, because a church is where you are supposed to be friendly and Christian and all. The Reverend Filbert went forward, and then Daddy, as I think he was proud of Mom's courage even though he regretted the circumstances. One by one other folks came up and spoke. They were not relaxed about it, but they made the effort.

And I, when I had recovered from my astonishment, loaded a paper plate with food, including the piece of fried chicken I had intended for myself, and bore it to Mr. King with the compliments of Mt. Carmel. Afterward, I went over to Mom and hugged her around the waist. I was proud she was my mom.

I was glad later that I did, for you will not believe what I tell you next. The Mt. Carmel congregation has its ways of getting at folks. They did not eat any of the food that Mom brought. No doubt you are wondering how it is possible to distinguish one person's cooking from another when it is available in such quantities, but there are plenty of people in Arnold's Corners who can walk up and down beside those tables and tell you exactly who cooked what.

It is a deep humiliation to a woman not to have most of her Homecoming food eaten up. I saw Mom looking every now and then at her dishes. She even went so far as to urge some of it on this person or that, but all she spoke to declined with some polite remark about having eaten so much they could just about pop. I ate bean salad and ham until I felt I had stashed a bushel, but I hardly dented the supply.

I do not know whether it was Judgment, but clouds began building up and by two o'clock the sky was dark and heavy. Unfortunately, the bottom dropped out before the food and dishes could be gathered together. I rushed Timmy to the car, then took the dishes and trays as Mom and Daddy handed them in to me one by one. Lightning flashed and thunder echoed through the woods back of the church. The rain roared on the car's roof. By the time they were safely inside the car, Mom and Daddy were soaked to the skin.

Mom's hair hung gray and limp—she looked exceedingly discouraged. Daddy was grim. We sat in silence —all but Timmy, who has never been silent in his life except when he was asleep. Sheets of rain whammed the car windows and made it impossible to see out.

120

"Are we going to leave Mr. King?" I asked in a small voice.

Daddy's jaw tightened. He started the car engine. "King seems to have gotten here without us."

"Tal," Mom said.

Daddy sighed and cut off the engine. "Open the window and see if you can find him," he said to me.

It was not easy to locate him with the rain pouring through the window into my face, but finally I saw him standing under a large oak. His shoulders were hunched against the rain. He had taken off the green jacket, folded it inside out, and tucked it under one arm. He was a forlorn sight.

"Haven't you ever been told not to stand under a tree in an electrical storm!" I shouted. "Come on. We're taking you home!"

He hesitated.

"Come *on!*" I said again just as lightning flashed. "I'm getting wet!"

He sat with the food and me. Timmy hung fascinated halfway over the back of the front seat. I asked as discreetly as I could if Mr. King had any encouraging words to say about his stolen property. He shook his head, and a mixture of sadness and anger showed in his eyes for a second or two. I had to bear the burden of conversation, as the three grown-ups were not inclined to talk to one another.

We let our passenger off a few minutes later at Mr. Lyman's driveway. He still had a walk ahead of him, but at least he could stand on Mr. Lyman's porch until the rain stopped. He thanked Daddy, who did not say he was welcome, being no hypocrite. Mom had the grace to mention she was glad to have met him. It was a bleak parting all around. I wondered what had pos-

121

sessed him to show up at the Mt. Carmel Homecoming.

My hope for an improvement in affairs at home and at Brigham's Store did not materialize. Daddy did not look well, but when I mentioned it to him he merely hitched up his pants and said there wasn't anything wrong with him. I tried to be extra nice to Mom, but it was hard to keep her spirits up, as she was still smarting under the burden of all the uneaten Homecoming food. The only bright spot in my life was the fact that Jenny was doing a beautiful job on Mrs. Crifton's dress. I felt pretty good, to think that I was responsible, even if nobody knew it but Mrs. Crifton and me.

The first thing to greet my eyes when I opened them early Wednesday morning was Mom leaning over me.

"Your daddy's sick," she whispered. "He's not able to get out of bed."

I sat straight up. "What's wrong?"

"I don't know. He has a high fever. You'll have to get up. There's lots to be done. Get on your bicycle and ride to Dr. Carey's. As soon as you get back, I'll go open the store. I'll try to keep things going there until a decent hour. Then maybe Randy Mitchell will come in to work. You can cook breakfast and feed Timmy—"

"Now, wait just a minute," I said. "I will be glad to do anything you say, but may I suggest a different plan?"

Mom's lips pressed together. "Rosalee, this is no time for fooling around."

"I know, but it will take me a long time to get to Dr. Carey's and back, whereas you could make the trip in fifteen minutes in the car."

"I don't like to leave your daddy," Mom said faintly.

"I can look after him for fifteen minutes," I assured

her. "And when you're back, I'll go open the store. After all, I know more about it than you do."

Mom put her hand out suddenly and touched my hair. "I guess I can begin to be grateful for all the days you've spent hanging around that place," she said.

I dressed and we went up to the bedroom where Daddy was lying under the covers. I had never seen him sick before. His complexion was gray, except for two pink spots on his cheeks. I counted about a hundred lines on his face that I had not noticed before.

"I'm going for the doctor, Tal," Mom said. "Rosalee will stay with you."

"I don't need anybody to stay with me."

"You do, too," I said in my cool business voice, to let him know his appearance did not alarm me—which it did. I was thankful Mom did not have to go all the way to Bent City. We have been lucky in Arnold's Corners that Doc Carey bought a farm here and settled down when he retired from the Army.

I spent most of the time wringing cold washcloths and putting them on Daddy's forehead. He let me, but I had the feeling he was just enduring because he knew it made me feel better to be doing something besides standing around looking at him. He was right. I will frankly say I was relieved when Mom took over again —she is better equipped for being a nurse. Dr. Carey was on his way, she said, and I could go open the store.

Daddy was not happy at the notion of me being in charge of his precious store, but he also knew that I knew more about it than Mom. It was a case of choosing the lesser of two amateurs. He finally granted me permission to take the store key ring and the money sack of bills and change for the cash register. I felt better than I had in days—here was a job that I could do. Such a state of affairs can do a lot to restore a girl's spirits.

The store was dark. The only light came through the front windows, which were too dingy to let in much. It is sort of scary, coming in alone.

First I put the money from the sack into the cash register drawer. Next I turned on the lights and the ceiling fans and opened the big front door. That's all there is to opening our store. Then you sit and wait for the customers to come, which in this case they didn't. My stomach growled. I ate the peanut-butter sandwich I had brought from home and drank a pint of chocolate milk. That is a strange breakfast, but filling.

By nine o'clock Brigham's Store had had all of two customers, and I had rung up a total of two dollars and thirty cents. That is not exactly a booming business day. I thought about that sign swinging over the gas pump—No CREDIT CARDS.

I went outside, pulled a box over to the gas pump, stood on it, and unhooked the sign. That done, I put the box back in place and walked away from the store to look at it with a more critical eye. Road dust caked the screens of the door and windows. A couple of faded, out-of-date Bent City movie posters leaned forward from the inside of the window of the old post office corner. There was a generally dark and unwelcome appearance about that window.

"Good grief!" I said out loud. "No wonder nobody stops!"

Obviously it was Providence that Daddy had taken sick. I knew if he were around, he would never consent to what I resolved to do. I was grateful, for once, for the lack of customers, as it gave me more time to work.

The very first thing was to clean up the post office

124

corner to make a place for R. D.'s Effervescent Mouth-wash in case Peter York should happen by again before Daddy recovered. The window was large and square, as I have mentioned, with a wide sill. A rickety table sat just under it. Cobwebs on the inside matched the dust from the road on the outside. I removed the old movie posters and the screen. For the next two hours, inside and out, I slung considerable water and soap. I had to climb up on the table and use a brush with a long handle to get at the worst of the grime in the up-permost corners. Looking out, I could see all the way down Widows Row.

I saw Mrs. Crifton making her steady way across the highway on foot toward our store. She had a large flat box under one arm. When she looked up and saw me in the window, she was so startled she almost walked into the side of a pickup truck coming along the highway. I made haste to get down from the window.

"I come for a loaf of bread," she said when she got inside the store and laid her box on the counter. "And I need a box of snuff and a bottle of liniment."

I fetched the things for her and put them in a sack.

"I just been to Jenny's," she said.

I clapped my hand over my mouth. In my zeal I had forgotten to send word to Jenny that I couldn't be there that morning!

"Jenny finished my dress. It's right pretty." She pointed to the flat box on the counter. " 'Course, I don't know how it looks on me, as I didn't try it on there. She don't have a full-length mirror like I do. She was won-derin' where you were—said you were so dependable she knew you must be sick, not to show up. That's why I was surprised to see you in the window like that, more or less expecting you to be home in the bed."

125

"It's Daddy that's sick," I managed to say. "He was taken in the night."

"Oh? He's bad off?"

"I don't know," I said, trying to sound usual. It was not easy, the way I felt. How could I have been so forgetful? "I had to leave the house before Dr. Carey could make a diagnosis."

Mrs. Crifton lost interest. She gathered up the sack in her arms and started out.

"If you'll be passing by Jenny's again, would you tell her why I couldn't come today, please?" I asked meekly.

"I might," was all she said.

I returned to the post office corner and resumed cleaning, but my heart was no longer in it. I had let Jenny down. Nobody had stopped for gasoline since I took down the sign. I was very hungry—the peanut-butter sandwich had long since been digested. After a while I gave up. The window sparkled in the sun and the post office corner gleamed, but that did not give me any great satisfaction.

While I looked around among the merchandise for something appetizing, I discovered that Mrs. Crifton had left the flat box on the counter—the box with her new dress inside.

I despaired. She would come back when she realized the oversight. I did not relish the return visit. She has a tendency to dampen my spirits. I was lifting the box to see how much it weighed when a familiar husky voice said quietly, "Hey, Rosalee!"

I whirled around.

May stood just outside the door, pressing her forehead against the screen to see in.

14

❖❖❖❖❖❖❖❖❖❖❖

I do not know when I have ever been so glad to see anybody. Her smile was as wide as mine.

"Get yourself in here right now!" I said. "Gosh—"

"I bet you thought I was dead." She grinned.

"No," I said, "but I did not think I would see you again before school started."

"In a little old place like Arnold's Corners?" May hooted. "There's not enough space to keep us separated!"

We looked at each other.

"I'm not supposed to have any truck with you," she admitted. "Mama let me come for some Pepsis because I told her you work mornings for Mrs. Chapman. Did you lose your job?"

I explained about Daddy's sickness. "And I don't know if I have lost my job or not," I sighed. "I forgot to let Jenny know I wouldn't be there today. She'll think she can't count on me anymore. A lot of people are feeling that way about me these days—especially my own Mom and Daddy."

"Your folks and mine are the same. I might have to mind them long as I live with 'em," May said grudgingly, "but I don't necessarily have to agree in my head."

My spirits soared. "You are right!" I exclaimed.

It is amazing what a little bit of comradeship can do for a low attitude. We drank Pepsis and ate sandwiches and talked. May told me about all that had happened to her in the time since our day at the creek. Bud, she said, was still angry with her. She had gotten the promised licking and still had marks on her legs to prove it. She had to stay in her own yard until today, except for going to Mr. Lewis' tobacco sheds to work.

"Times has been dull," she said. "Mama wouldn't even let me ride Baby Doll. I had to walk up here today."

"I'm sorry for the trouble I got you into," I said.

"It's not your fault," May said. "Nobody leads me around."

That made me feel a little better. I told her about Daddy's declining business and about our being snubbed for two Sundays in a row at Mt. Carmel. I told her about salesmanship and selling exclusiveness to Mrs. Crifton. I told her about Mr. King meeting Jenny and drawing her picture, and about the sketch pad being stolen. May listened to all I had to say. It is very heartening to be listened to, for once.

"Gosh!" she said. "You sure do lead a exciting life!"

I had not thought of it in that way. "It only seems so when I tell it to you, because you are interested. Anyway, I have about decided not to try to sell Jenny's dress designing. Peter York says you need a display of the product to grab the public's attention, and I do not have any of Jenny's work to display. We will just have to wait until Mrs. Crifton's daughter gets married and—"

My eye fell upon the flat box.

"What's the matter?" May asked warily. "You got that funny look in your eye."

I raised my right hand and pointed a finger at the ceiling. "May—Providence has placed a golden opportunity in our laps."

May was unmoved. She is of a more practical nature than I am, if you can imagine it. "I think I will be going home," she said.

"Look—this is Mrs. Crifton's sky-blue linen gown," I explained, grabbing up the box and thrusting it under her nose. "It is the most beautiful dress anybody in Arnold's Corners ever owned, and how can you explain it as anything but Providence when Mrs. Crifton herself, who *never* comes to our store and especially lately, came this very morning and left her precious gown on this very counter!"

"So?" said May.

"So—we've got the product! Before we return it to Mrs. Crifton, we are going to show this gown to Arnold's Corners!"

I could tell by May's expression that she thought I had gone crazy, but she was not willing to leave me in that condition, being a true friend.

"How?" she asked in a hushed voice. "And where do you get this 'we' business?"

I took her hand and pulled her over to the post office corner. "Providence again. I spent the entire morning cleaning the place up." I pointed to the sparkling window. "I didn't even understand it myself at the time."

"I don't understand it now," May said.

"Look," I said, leaping upon the rickety table and from there to the windowsill. "When I stand here I can be seen by anybody who passes."

"Yeah," May nodded. "And they got a mental hospital for people who act like you are acting now."

"Furthermore," I said, jumping to the floor, "while I'm up in that window, I'll be wearing Mrs. Crifton's dress!"

"Rosalee! You have lost what's left of your mind— I'm leaving this place right now."

I grabbed May's arm. "May, think of Jenny and Daddy. They both need help in their businesses. People will come in the store today to give me orders for exclusive outfits, and while they're here, they'll buy stuff. Daddy will be astounded. And Jenny will have more orders than she can fill, and she'll start making enough money to live on. She'll need both you *and* me to baby-sit!"

That point had more weight with May. She was not so interested in the economic problems of Daddy or Jenny, but she loves babies.

"You can't wear Mrs. Crifton's dress," she stalled. "She would make eight of you."

"It'll have to be pinned," I said, going to the sewing notions shelf and taking out some straight pins. "I have looked at the window displays of the Exclusive Shoppe in Bent City. It doesn't matter if the dress is not the same size as the dummy—they pin it all up in the back, so it looks good in the front."

May was alarmed. "That'll wrinkle the dress—and make pinholes in it!"

"Not if we do it right," I said. "First thing, I'll make a

130

sign." I took one of the old movie posters, turned it to the blank side, and used a grease pencil to write:

EXCLUSIVE ORIGINAL
by J. CHAPMAN, DESIGNER
ORDER YOURS TODAY!
Inquire Within

I stuck the poster in the window with Scotch tape. We took the dress out of the box at last. May held the top while I got underneath the wide skirt and let it fall over my head.

The problems were obvious right away. The sky-blue formal had a scooped-out neckline designed for a large expanse of chest, which I do not have. I decided I'd better keep my shirt on, regardless of the effect.

May was more concerned about the dress than about me, and as her hands were shaking, she stuck me several times during the pinning process.

"I'm leavin' with my Pepsis soon as I get you in this thing," she mumbled through a mouthful of pins. "I'm not going to be anywhere around when the ax falls." When I did not respond right away, she added, "I been wondering how you plan to climb up on the table once I'm finished."

I had not thought of that. Vaulting upon tables is not too difficult when you are wearing shorts, but skirts complicate things somewhat. I finally made a stair-step arrangement of soft-drink crates that I could maneuver if I held the skirt.

"Now," I said, "I'm getting up in the window. If anybody comes in, you can wait on them."

May looked stricken. "I can't do that! I don't know how much things cost or how to work the cash register!"

"The only other choice is for you to wear the dress and stand in the window!" I said.

"That's no kind of choice!" May argued.

"I will open the cash register," I said, mashing the button. The drawer clanged open. "All you have to do is give the proper change. Don't even bother to ring up the amount."

The first thing I did after making my way up the drink-crate steps was to look out the window to see whether Mrs. Crifton might be coming back. She wasn't. I did not want her to see me in her dress. As soon as she loomed, I could get down, have May unpin me, fold the dress, remove the poster, and be my normal self before Mrs. Crifton arrived at the store. The sun was bright, the sky was blue, and there was plenty of traffic. I was bound to be noticed.

Modeling clothes is alien to my character, so I tried to recall how the dummies in the Exclusive Shoppe were posed. I stood sideways and put my left hand on my hip and my right hand up in the air. One side of the neckline slipped off my shoulder. I tugged it back in place.

I counted to one hundred and twenty. The arm in the air got heavier and heavier. I glanced over my shoulder at May standing stiffly by the cash register. She was not happy.

"Don't worry!" I told her. She was not comforted.

I turned again to look out the window. A long black car was just passing, heading east. A pickup truck was coming from the opposite direction. As the driver of the car glanced in the direction of Brigham's Store, I let my numb right hand drop and put up the left.

The driver looked, looked away, and looked again, this time with his mouth open and eyes staring. That's how I remember his face. The long black car swerved and skidded, and right before my horrified eyes the truck and the car sideswiped each other with a sickening scrape of metal on metal.

In the silence afterward I could not move. Then my knees began to give way. May caught my elbow and helped me from the table.

"What have I done?" I exclaimed. "What have I done!"

"Just hush your mouth and stand still so I can get you out of this thing!" May said grimly. She unpinned the dress. Despite the fact that we were both trembling from head to foot, we managed to get the dress folded and back into the box before all the people began pouring into the store.

I do not know where they came from. You would have thought that every person in Berry County was waiting in the ditches along the roadside for this moment to occur. I looked out the front door and my heart skipped a beat. Cars were backed up behind cars in both directions. Horns honked and the hot sun gleamed on metal. Had anyone been hurt? What was I supposed to do? I had seen the wreck happen. I had *caused* it!

It was probably lucky that May and I were caught up in the rush of waiting on customers. Both of us would gladly have fled forever if there had been a way to do so. The cash register bell rang steadily. The drawer was soon stuffed with bills and coins.

The highway patrolman arrived and soon had traffic moving again around the two wrecked vehicles. I was relieved to hear that no one had been hurt and that the truck and car would be able to drive away under their own power. The customers began leaving, until at last there was no one left in the store but May and me.

133

And the highway patrolman. He filled up the doorway in his smart uniform and wide-brimmed hat. May's people have never been overly fond of the uniformed law. She was frankly terrified, and my business face would not go in place for any amount of effort on my part.

"Hello, young ladies," he said, removing his hat. "I'm Trooper Woolridge. May I speak to the person in charge?"

I swallowed hard. "I'm Rosalee Brigham. My daddy owns the store, but he's sick in bed today. I'm running things." I did not introduce him to May, as I thought she would like it better if I did not.

He looked down at a piece of paper he had in his hand. "I see," he said. "Well—were you here when the accident occurred?"

I nodded. I was sure he could see my knees trembling.

He looked around the store, noting the window. "I don't suppose you saw the actual accident, did you?"

What could I say? While I was trying to frame the words, he went on.

"The gentleman driving the car said he was distracted by some sort of strange statue in the window of this store. No one else seems to have seen it, but I thought I'd ask about witnesses anyway, for the report."

He folded the piece of paper and put it in his pocket. "Would you sell a trooper a cold drink before he carries on his duties?"

I nodded. He was very friendly, but talking was hard. May said, "I got to go home now." She walked out without the drinks her mama had sent her to get. I had to call her back.

When she was gone at last, there was nobody but me and Trooper Woolridge. I rang up the quarter he gave me for the drink and gave him change. I also made a resolution.

"Sir," I said, and my voice sounded like somebody else's, far, far away. "I have got to tell you something."

It did not take long to explain to him. He listened to every word. I do not know whether he would ever have believed me, but I showed him the poster that had been in the window, and Mrs. Crifton chose that moment to come back to Brigham's Store, having missed all the excitement. After she finally waddled away with her flat box, he knew I was telling the truth.

15

✿✿✿✿✿✿✿✿✿✿✿✿

Trooper Woolridge discreetly waited until Mrs. Crifton's departure, then thanked me for speaking up, which made me feel worse than ever. He finished his drink and set the empty bottle on the counter.

"I'll include what you've told me in my report. It'll probably be a matter of settlement between the insurance companies. I doubt it'll go to court, since nobody was injured or killed and the vehicles weren't badly damaged."

I followed him to the door. "When will I know?"

"Probably in the next day or so. Don't worry about it."

It was easy for him to say that. What was I going to tell Daddy, who had surely already heard about the accident from the neighbors and was probably gnashing his teeth? Moreover, what would happen if Mrs. Crifton found out that her dress had been worn in the window of our store before she ever had a chance to try it on? And May—as far as she was concerned, I was

Trouble with a capital *T*. Would she ever trust me again as long as she lived?

I went home that evening with a burdened conscience. I told Daddy only that I happened to be in the post office window when the accident occurred and might be called to court as a witness. I did not elaborate, as that report alone caused him to turn pale and groan loudly. He did not ask why I was in the window. Maybe he was afraid to hear the answer. I did not reap much joy from handing him the extra-heavy money sack, even though Brigham's had had the best business day in two weeks.

Daddy's sickness was caused by a virus, Mom told me, and he had to stay in bed until completely recovered. It would be my job to keep store in the meantime. Jenny was willing to do without my baby-sitting services. There was nothing for me to do but agree, although I had a strong urge to pack my few treasures in a sack and leave Arnold's Corners forever, before the roof caved in.

Which I fully expected. I lived in fear of Judgment. I did not see how it could be possible that with all the people who had appeared so suddenly after the wreck, no one had seen me in the window in Mrs. Crifton's dress. Someone was bound to come forward at any moment. I feared that Mrs. Crifton herself would discover pinholes in her brand-new gown and come to our door seeking restitution. I feared that someone would put the finger on me as the cause of the accident, in spite of Trooper Woolridge's assurances that a driver is not supposed to allow himself to be distracted. I had visions of his coming around to tell me that the case would go to court after all and that I must appear as a witness. Of course, if I did so, the whole story of me and the dress would come to light in the Bent City *Times*.

What I dreaded most of all, though, was that Jenny might learn what a foolish thing I had done with the beautiful gown she had worked so hard to make. She has treated me like a grown-up always, but she would have second thoughts, after this.

Daddy was somewhat irked when Saturday came and he still was not allowed to get out of bed. He had no choice but to let me mind the store.

"I want you to get word to Randy Mitchell to come and help you out," he said as I took the keys from him, but I did not promise.

I recalled how a lull in business had gotten me into trouble just three days before, so to keep out of mischief I took along one of the Bookmobile books. Mrs. Chips was due back in Arnold's Corners soon, and I had not finished my allotted number.

About eleven o'clock I sat down on the step stool we use for reaching the high shelves and opened my book on the counter. I could not concentrate. There is something about that store when it is empty of people. The clock buzzes. The ice-cream cabinet hums. There is always at least one wasp singing back and forth across the ceiling. I fidgeted and read the same sentences over several times. At the bottom of page two I heard a scratching noise on the other side of the stock room door.

The hair prickled at the back of my neck. I closed the book and sat there for a minute. Probably a rat or a mouse, I told myself.

"Why, hello, Mr. Purdy!" I said loudly to the empty store. My voice was more high-pitched than I would have liked. "Sure am glad you dropped by! It gets lonesome sometimes."

The scratching broke off. Now, I thought, a rat will start gnawing again. Minutes passed. The sound did not come again. Finally I got up and began to ease toward the front, all the time keeping an eye on the stock room door.

Between one eye-blink and the next, the heavy, gray, plank door opened, a very tiny crack. I saw one wide-open, pleading eye in a dark face, and the door shut again quietly.

It was May!

I almost cried from pure relief. The next minute I was with her in the dim feed-smelling room.

"I can't believe you're here!" I choked, grabbing her arm. "I thought . . . I thought you'd never want to see me again after Wednesday . . ."

"What kind of a friend do you think I am?" May asked.

"You nearly scared me out of my wits," I said. "Why did you hide in here instead of coming in the front door?"

"I ain't even supposed to be *close* to here. I'm supposed to be at Aunt Gloria's this minute pickin' peaches. Aunt Gloria thinks I'm home—Mama thinks I'm to Aunt Gloria's." She looked at the ceiling. "It'll be a great day Sunday morning when they get together at church and find out I never was at either place!"

It was beyond my understanding that May Thomas could be so foolhardy, as that is more one of my failings than one of hers. "Look," I said, "if you don't watch out, your folks won't trust you anymore. I know. It's not worth it just to be able to say you put something over on them."

May's eyes flashed. "Do you think I'd risk myself and come all the way here for a joke? I've a good mind to leave right now and let things happen like they going to!" She folded her arms across her chest and looked away.

I had hurt her feelings, and I was sorry. "What's the matter, May?"

Her eyes got very serious. We sat down on one of the full sacks. "They going to do something mean to Mr. King," she said in a low voice. "I come to tell you, so you can get your daddy to stop them."

I felt myself getting cold all over. "Who's going to do something to him—and what are they going to do? How'd you find out?"

She took a deep breath. "Down at Mr. Lewis' tobacco shed yesterday morning. We was all of us working and talking, like we do, and all of a sudden that long red car of Bill Steed's comes screeching up in a dust cloud. He jumps out—ups to Mr. Lewis and says right out, 'You all set for the big party tomorrow night?'

"Mr. Lewis looks over toward us and we pretend like we're not payin' attention, but we are, and he says something under his breath to Bill Steed.

"Bill laughs that loud laugh of his and says, 'Oh, it don't matter if they hear—what can they do about it? They don't care if white folks kill each other off!' And Randolph Larue right next to me says 'Right on!' but not loud enough anybody but me can hear.

"And I say under my breath, 'Shut your mouth, Randolph! Who they talkin' about?' And he says, 'I don't know for sure, but I think that hippie man been hangin' around Mr. Lyman's. And maybe Mr. Lyman too.'

"I can't tell you nothin' else," she finished, turning her pale palms up. "I did my best to find out without

140

seemin' to, but all I know is, Mr. Lewis and Bill Steed and the Lord knows who are planning something for tonight. I tried and tried to figure a way to get to you last night, but this was the best I could do."

I did not know what to say. May put a hand on my arm.

"I don't want to see anything happen to Mr. King," she said simply. "You tell your daddy and he—"

"But Daddy's still sick in bed!" I burst out. "He's not even supposed to get up. That's why I'm here."

May's face clouded over. "Looks like I came for nothin' then, don't it?"

"No," I said, standing up. "You did the right thing. You probably saved Mr. King's life."

She brightened. "You mean you already got a plan?"

I paced the little bare square of concrete floor. "No," I admitted, "but I will have before the day is over."

"Hey!" A voice boomed suddenly from the other side of the door. "Anybody around here?"

May's whole aspect collapsed. "That's Mr. Lewis—I recognize his voice," she whispered.

"Shhh! Stay put while I go see what he wants. He'll never know you're here."

I put on my cool business face and slipped through the stock room door into the store. Bonnie's daddy was leaning on the counter, drumming upon it with his fingers.

"How do, Red," he said formally. "Where's your daddy?"

"He's sick in bed. What can I do for you?" I kept telling myself not to be scared, but my self would not listen. He couldn't know that May was in the stock room, or that I knew what he and Bill were up to. Or could he? I hoped I looked plain.

"He's letting you run the store." It was more a statement than a question, and it implied my daddy did not have good sense. That angered me somewhat.

"Yes," I said.

"Well, I come for some hog feed," he said, after a moment.

"I'll get it for you," I said, edging back to the stock room.

"Fifty-pound sack," he said, standing up to come with me. "I doubt you can lift it. I'll help."

"I can get it," I said between my teeth. It probably sounded rude, but I could not let him find May crouched among the sacks. "I will call out to you if I find I can't lift it after all," I amended as I let myself into the stock room. I shut the door quickly and latched it, in case Mr. Lewis should take it in his mind to help anyway.

May had not moved.

"You've got to get out of here right now!" I whispered. "Don't walk in the open until the coast is clear, because if Mr. Lewis sees you, he'll put two and two together and—"

She nodded. "I'll go back the way I came. I'm going to hide in that clump of woods back of the store till he's gone, then I'll cross down back of Aunt Gloria's field."

"Be careful," I said as she slipped out. "And thanks. You're a real friend." She flashed me a smile and was gone.

It took a moment for me to collect myself and remember that I was fetching a sack of hog feed for Mr. Lewis.

Blam! Blam! Blam! He was pounding on the gray door now. "Are you gonna fetch me that feed or have I got to go to Bent City for it?" he hollered.

"Coming!" I puffed. I found what he wanted and half dragged, half carried it toward the door. I have read in books that when a person is frightened his adrenalin glands work overtime and he is able to perform physical feats that are ordinarily impossible. I do not believe it. I thought I would never make it to the door, but I did, finally, and fumbled the latch open.

"Here you are," I said. I did not know if my business face was on or not. I did not really care. All I wanted was for him to leave so I could think.

"How much?" he said, giving me a curious look.

"I don't know," I gulped. "I'll write it in the book and you can settle with Daddy when he comes in next week."

"I thought I might see him tonight," Mr. Lewis said, heaving the huge sack up to his shoulder with no sign of effort. I noted the size of his muscles and winced.

"Oh, no," I said. "I don't think that'd be wise—he's got a virus. It would be catching. He has to stay in be . . ."

My voice trailed off. Why did Mr. Lewis think he might see Daddy tonight? I stared. Mr. Lewis gave me one last curious look, turned on his heel, and walked out.

16

❁❁❁❁❁❁❁❁❁❁❁❁

I could not stop trembling. Worse than that, though, was the fact that my mind wouldn't work, which has hardly ever been the case since I was born. Mr. King had to be warned—and I would have to do it. I didn't know anybody who could be trusted.

Not even my own daddy.

I tried to put that thought out of my mind, but it stubbornly persisted. Mr. Lewis had said he thought he might see Daddy tonight. Did he mean my daddy was mixed up in the scheme too? Surely not. My daddy would never have anything to do with Bill Steed's ideas.

Still, he certainly hadn't been himself lately. I had thought he had acted funny because he was coming down with the virus, but now I began to wonder—had he been pretending to be sick all this time? No—that was ridiculous—he couldn't fool Doc Carey.

Unless Doc Carey was in on it too. Maybe they were

going to furnish alibis for each other. Maybe every able-bodied man in Arnold's Corners . . .

"I have been reading too many books!" I said aloud. Regardless of who was involved, I had to get to Mr. King's camper before dark. Daddy liked to close the store at seven o'clock on Saturdays. It would still be fairly light at seven, but I could not wait that long to start out. I debated making a call to the Highway Patrol but thought better of it. Who would believe a half-grown girl when she says that a bunch of respectable citizens are about to do something unrespectable? I had no proof. In books the police always have to have proof before they can do official acts. Also, considering the circumstances of my recent acquaintance with Trooper Woolridge, I doubted that he would take me seriously.

There is no way to describe how I felt when Randy Mitchell came strolling into the store about five o'clock.

"Boy, am I ever glad to see you!" I said. I am afraid I was too fervent. He gave me a suspicious look. Randy is seventeen and has lots of wavy blond hair. He uses hair tonic. We despise each other thoroughly. He knows I have never been glad to see him in my life.

"Well, I cannot say the same," he told me. "Give me two cartons of Pepsis."

I was humiliated, but I had to get Randy to keep store for me, even if I had to pay him out of my own savings.

"I guess you heard Daddy's sick," I ventured, taking my time with the drinks.

"Naw."

"Yeah. He's got a virus."

Randy shrugged. "Lotta people get that."

"I really need to be home with Mom—so near to sup-pertime, with him sick," I said. "She worries about the store, though. I sure would appreciate it if you'd keep store for me—us—until seven o'clock closing time, so I could be at home to help."

Randy turned very slowly and gave me an indescrib-able look. After a minute he drawled, "I sure *bet* you'd appreciate it. I bet you'd appreciate it so much you'd even make an excuse I could tell this cute little Bent City girl for why I had to break my date with her!"

"Well, you wouldn't have to spend the night here! I told you we close at seven."

"I got to get ready, though," Randy said, feeling the fuzz on his chin. "That takes a while, me having to shave and all. I'm supposed to pick her up at seven thirty." Then he acted like he was disgusted at himself for saying that much to me. "Hurry up with them drinks or I'll wait on myself!"

I rang up the money he gave me. "How much does Daddy pay you when you work for him?"

"None of your business. He took the two full cartons, one in each hand, and started out.

"I'll pay you twice what he would," I said.

Randy stopped in his tracks and turned back to face me.

"You could have twice as good a date if you had twice the money," I raced on. "After all, this girl's from Bent City. She's not going to be interested in any old cheap evening at a movie with one bag of popcorn—you got to show her something different. I bet nobody's ever taken her out to eat at a restaurant on a date. You could do that, if you had the money. She will know you are a man of the world by the fact that you invite her to dinner at eight o'clock, which is very high class."

146

I stopped for breath. Randy gave me a pained look.

"How much does Daddy pay you?" I asked again, and prayed I had the amount to match it.

"Dollarnaquarter a hour," he said.

I did some quick figuring. Five to seven o'clock, two hours, two fifty per hour.

"I'll pay you five dollars in advance to stay here until seven and close up for me," I told him. "How about it?"

He did not want to give in too soon, but I knew I had him. "How come you're so anxious to get home? I never knew you to be especially fond of helping around the house." He has heard Daddy and me have words on the subject.

"I am a changed person," I said. "My father is ill and my poor mother has to bear the load of his illness as well as care for my rambunctious baby brother. I feel it is my duty to be at home with her in her hour of trial."

"You don't have to lay it on so thick!" Randy said. "Where's the five dollars?"

We understood each other. I took a five-dollar bill out of the register and gave it to him, making a note to myself to replace it out of the cigar-box savings under my bed. Ten minutes later I was on my way out of the door, with plenty of time to get to Mr. King and warn him to leave.

I took my time pedaling along and was lost in thought about strategy when Les Barton's oldest look-alike son, Junior, passed me on his bike heading in the other direction.

"Hey, Red! Where you going?"

If lightning had hit me from the blue skies, I could not have been more startled. The Bartons had been in our store the day Bill Steed insulted Mr. King. No doubt Mr. Barton and his crowd were not to be trusted either.

"To Hooker's . . . for a stamp!" I said, breezing right on by.

It is not good to be caught in a lie, especially if you are acting as a sort of secret agent. I had a dime in my jeans, so I could buy a stamp if push came to shove. And I did have to pass Hooker's on my way to Mr. Lyman's. Also, I might be able to overhear something that had bearing on the case.

I must admit it irritated me somewhat, when I got inside the little old crampy store, to see some of Daddy's former best customers standing around drinking soft drinks and talking. Conversation came to a halt when I walked in the door.

I felt most peculiar, but would never let any of them know that. I had on my best cool business face. I gazed neither to the right nor to the left, but went straight to Mr. Hooker, who was on the far side of the counter.

"A-law, Red! You comin' to ask for that job again, now your daddy's business is not doing so well?"

I purely despised him for that. "My daddy's business is doing quite well, thank you."

"Whatcha want?" he asked, grinning and grinning.

"A stamp," I said, fingering the dime in my pocket.

"Well, I tell you what, Red," he said. He put both fat hands on the counter and hunched his elbows out and leaned toward me. "I don't suppose you remember this, it's been so long since you had occasion to deal with the situation, but the Federal Post Office window closes at noon on Saturday. Much as I'd like to, I can't sell you no stamp."

I could have kicked myself clean out of the door,

unaided. It is hard to maintain your dignity under such circumstances.

"I see," I said, lifting my chin. "I'm sorry to have bothered you."

I turned and went out. I did not know whether my face was red, white, or blue. Where being mortified is concerned, that was truly the high point in my life, so far.

I am sure it was not later than five forty when I got to Mr. Lyman's. His rusty mailbox leaned out toward the highway like the head of a frozen turkey. Grass, chickweed, bramble bushes, Queen Anne's lace, chinaberry trees, and morning glory vines ran one another a close race to see which could do the best job of hiding his house from people passing.

The house had a closed-up look, but I wasn't sure whether it was because Mr. Lyman was not home, or because his personality had rubbed off on the place. I laid the bike on its side and picked my way through the weeds to the porch.

Nobody answered my knock. I waited and waited. Cars zoomed by on the highway. I wondered how near six o'clock it was getting to be.

I began to feel uneasy. I had been counting on Mr. Lyman's help in locating Mr. King. Common sense told me, of course, that the camper was parked somewhere deep in the woods, but I had never been in those woods from this direction. I would have a considerable journey to make into unknown territory. I had some vague remembrance about moss growing on the north side of trees, but have never been sure how that helps a person find his way.

I wheeled the bike around to the back of the house

to study the lay of the land. The driveway was part of a road that passed the house and the cornfield beyond. The road had been worn by truck and tractor wheels—the wheel ruts were separated by a middle mound of grass and weeds. When it got to the edge of the woods, the road divided into two narrower roads. I chose the one to the right.

The pedaling wasn't too rough at first because I stayed in the wheel ruts. After a while, though, the road became a footpath. You could see where trucks came to a certain spot and turned around. I kept going. I went down a hill and around a curve and up another hill, and then all of a sudden the path wasn't there anymore. I was just making my way between trees.

I came to a standstill, having at last to admit that I had made a wrong choice and wasted valuable time. It is a heart-squeezing feeling to know you are going to be late for something important. There was nothing to do but turn around, go back to the fork in the road, and take the other way.

The light in the woods had turned red-gold. The air was cooler. It seemed forever ago since I left the store.

I have noticed that when I am not familiar with the territory I am traveling in, things look different on the way back from what they do going. I noticed little paths jutting off from the one I was on. I began to wonder if one of those might not be the one I should take. My legs trembled, whether from overwork or other reasons was hard to tell. Sweat collected in beads on my forehead and dripped down the side of my face. I had my own personal cloud of flies and bugs, one of which got in my right eye. It hurt! Tears ran down and mixed with the sweat.

The woods were very quiet. I thought how nice it

would be if somebody—anybody—would happen by. I would have welcomed the sight of Bill Steed, even!

I have read in books of people going mad when lost in the wilderness, and although I did not put much store by it originally, I do now, having been in that situation myself. The sky above the trees began to deepen in color. Just when I was convinced that I was completely and utterly lost, I rounded a tree and there I was, back at the fork of the road. This time I had to be right.

I tore off down the other road. Now I could see that this one was more traveled. The mound in the middle was not so deep in weeds. As a matter of fact, it was easier to ride the mound than the ruts, which is what I did. That is why, in my haste, I did not see the hole until it was too late. My front wheel plunged into it and the back wheel flipped up. I went over the handlebars, and my head slammed into something hard.

17

❀❀❀❀❀❀❀❀❀❀❀

I wanted to lie down and sleep, but somebody kept punching me in the upper arm and grabbing me by the chin and wobbling my head back and forth.

"Leave me alone!" I said. At least, that's what I tried to say, but it came out mushy.

"Come on, little girl. Open your eyes now. Come on."

I do not like to be referred to as "little girl," but the man's voice was kindly. I opened my eyes to see who it was. Little stabs of lightning went all through my skull. I was sitting up on a sofa. The man who owned the voice was leaning close to my face, peering at me. He seemed to be studying my eyes. It was somebody I knew—I tried to remember his name. He was elderly, with a ruddy, lined face.

"Don't you know me?" he asked. "I'm Lyman Hayes."

It was such a relief not to have to figure it out for myself that I closed my eyes again. It was strange, not being able to think or remember, even when I was trying with all my might. My head was heavy and sore.

I heard his footsteps moving around. "Hate to go off and leave you alone," he muttered, "but you got to have a doctor."

I opened my eyes again. "Do you live here?" My tongue felt as though it had been stuffed with foam rubber.

"Well, sure I live here!" he answered. "Don't you remember anything?"

I tried to oblige, but my brain would not take hold. "How . . . did I get here?"

He frowned. "You walked. Don't you even recollect that?"

I shook my head, and that made the lightning start popping again.

"Yep," he said, "I was coming to check on my traps, and I saw you flying along the road there on your bicycle. I was about to call out to you to watch out for that hole, but I never got the chance. You say you don't remember walking back here to the house with me? I rolled your bent-up bicycle. You claimed you weren't hurt too much—"

"No." All I wanted was to lay my aching head on something soft so I could go to sleep. I did not care about anything else.

"What in the world were you doin' on my road anyhow? You could of laid there all night and nobody would of known. A car coming in the dark wouldn't of seen you until it was too late—King could of run right over you, bicycle and all!"

King! The name jarred. I squinted, trying to think. The world was a very fuzzy place.

"Wh—where . . . is . . . Mr. King?" I asked finally.

"I don't have no idea."

"Tell . . . him—"

"Tell who? You mean King?"

I nodded. It began to come back to me in bits and pieces. I knew time was important. The heart-squeezed feeling returned.

"What . . . time . . . is it?" I tried to stand up.

He made me sit again. "Sun's gone down, but it still ain't dark. It's been about half an hour since we got back here. You must of knocked your brains loose on that piece of quartz in the road. Your forehead bled from where you cut it, and you got a goose egg up in your hair. Do your folks know where you're at?"

I wished he would not ask questions and talk. It made me forget what I had to tell him.

"Mr. King . . ." I said, with my eyes shut because that felt better. "He has . . . to leave." I remembered something else I had almost forgotten. "And you too."

"What in the world are you talking about, girl?"

"Bill Steed . . ." That name popped into my mind with no effort, and with it the way his face looked—freckled, round, and oily. I opened my eyes to get rid of the vision and saw instead Mr. Lyman's face looking grim and puzzled.

"They're planning something . . . bad," I said, squinting back at him. "For tonight. I . . . was going to . . . warn him . . . and you. I got . . . lost."

Mr. Lyman was dead serious. "Hon, is this some kind of little girl's game you are playing, or are you telling me the truth?"

"I do not . . . play . . . little girl's . . . games!" I said as firmly as I could under the circumstances. But that was not true—I knew I had been behaving like a silly child. I began to feel hopeless. No grown-up ever took stock in what I said, except Mr. King, and it looked

154

as though he would not have another chance now. Time had run out—and because I had tried to be some kind of hero I had not helped anybody. Tears rolled out of the corners of my eyes and dripped into my lap.

Mr. Lyman's worried expression did not help my feelings.

"Now, look, Girl. Everything is going to be all right, soon as I get the doctor and your ma and pa—"

"No, it isn't!" I sobbed. "Probably Mr. King is done for, this very minute—and they'll come for you next."

It was an effort, but I told him as much as I could remember of what May had seen at the tobacco shed the day before. I told him about Mr. Lewis' odd remark at the store that morning. I mentioned the stolen drawings, which he had not known about, having been away for several days. He was angry. He paced up and down the whole time I talked.

"If what you say is so, I need to get the law," he said when I had finished. "You stay right there. Lie down, flat on your back, and don't you try to get up till I've got the doctor to you. I don't know how loose your brains are. It might be if you try to move around you're liable to die." He started out, then added, "On the other hand, try not to go to sleep either. Might not wake up." And on that cheery note he was gone.

Mr. Lyman is old, I thought. He will stumble on a rock and fall on his head. If he finds Bill Steed—or Bill finds him—he will get it right between the eyes. I lay on my side and closed my eyes to rest them.

I came to, suddenly, scared.

For a few minutes I just lay in the dark listening to my heart pound and pound, trying to think. I *could* think, which I took as a sign of improvement. I remembered that I was at Mr. Lyman's house, and that he had left to get help. He had warned me not to go to sleep and not to get up because of my loosened brains. I reached up and felt my forehead. It was crusty with dried blood.

The room was terribly quiet. How long had Mr. Lyman been gone? It had not seemed so dark when I had closed my eyes. Had I gone to sleep, or passed out? What if Mr. Lyman had gone into his woods first, to see whether Mr. King was there in one piece? I imagined Mr. Lyman being ambushed by Bill Steed, and Bill learning from him, somehow, that I knew everything and was lying helpless on Mr. Lyman's living room sofa.

Suddenly I knew why I was scared.

I was not going to lie and wait for Bill Steed to come and get me! I was going home! I swung my legs over the side of the sofa and pushed myself to a sitting position. Lightning popped around inside my head for several seconds thereafter. I very nearly lost my resolution. My head weighed about forty pounds, which is a considerable burden if you are not used to it.

When I stood I almost fell. Green fog settled in my eyes, and I wondered how I was going to see my way. I stood very still until the fog went away and my eyes were used to the dark, then I moved slowly toward the shape of a door with my hands stretched out before me. I did not wish to knock my poor head against anything else.

The first door was standing open and led into a little hallway. I felt along the walls until my hands touched a doorknob. I turned it and prayed that Mr. Lyman hadn't locked me in. There was a satisfying click and a rush of cooler air as the door opened.

156

Beyond the weeds and vegetation an occasional headlight flared on the highway and disappeared. Traffic was not heavy. Maybe I could make it after all.

My heavy head seemed determined to roll off my neck if I bent it even slightly, so I held onto one of the porch posts and felt my way down the steps by foot. I never realized how painful the mere act of walking could be. My feet kept coming down in the wrong place—either too soon, because the ground was closer than I thought, or too late, because it was farther away. And every time my foot slammed against the ground my head swam in a pool of pain. It got so bad I was sick to my stomach. Afterward I leaned against a tree. Maybe Mr. Lyman was right—something was coming undone in my head and I was about to die.

When Dread creeps up on you, it is better to ignore the feeling and do something active. I struggled on. By putting one foot in front of the other I managed to get quite a way down the highway before I heard the sound of a vehicle approaching. The first thing that crossed my mind was that one of Bill Steed's crowd was arriving late for the "party." I had gotten away from Mr. Lyman's house just in time. That in itself was enough to make a girl weak in the knees if she was not already, which I was. I barely had time to scramble into the ditch before the oncoming headlight beams swept the road where I had been stumbling along.

After the car had passed, I peered up over the edge of the ditch. It was not a car at all, but a pickup truck, and it turned into Mr. Lyman's driveway. I could not tell whose truck it might be. Even as I speculated, it swung out into the highway again, headed back toward Arnold's Corners. I ducked.

I do not remember much about that long walk except

157

that every time I heard a car coming along the highway from either direction, I would lie in the ditch until it had gone by. It seemed to me that I was forever in the ditch, and then again it seemed I was stumbling forever along the roadside. I don't remember the getting up or getting down. I almost went to sleep once in the ditch, but a stray dog happened along and licked my face. When I rose up it frightened him off. I must have looked a sight, even to a stray dog who has probably seen everything there is to see.

It was a relief to get to Hooker's Store—at least now there would be houses. But the lights were out at Hooker's. Lights were on in most of the houses I passed after that, but there was no sign of life out of doors. I began to feel that I was alone in the world. When our store came into view at long last, I knew how strugglers on the desert feel when they see an oasis. It certainly gives the spirit a new lease on life. A person could almost cry.

But something was wrong.

Every light in the store was on, and more than a dozen cars and trucks were parked around the place. As I looked, two more drove up from the opposite direction and the drivers jumped out and ran into the store almost before the engines died.

Daddy would not like that at all! I should have known better than to trust Randy Mitchell. More than likely he had walked out of the store at seven o'clock with his precious five dollars and had not even bothered to turn out the lights and lock up! I was furious. That, apparently, is when my adrenalin does its flowing—when I am mad. Disregarding the pain in my head, I covered the ground between me and the store in a matter of minutes. No telling what was going on inside with nobody there to supervise! How many unpaid-for Pepsis would have to be accounted for, and how many cigarette butts had been ground into the floor?

The rumble of voices greeted my ears—it sounded like a Grange meeting or something. I flung open the screen door and stepped inside, letting it slam behind me. I think every man in Arnold's Corners was in our store. I saw Bill Steed, Les Barton, Mr. Hooker, Mr. Lyman, Doc Carey, and . . . yes . . . even Mr. King. They were all standing around Trooper Woolridge. All eyes turned in my direction. I do not know who was the more astounded—them or me. Something inside my head was pounding to get out. I looked around for Daddy. There was no sign of him.

"This store," I said thickly, "is *supposed* to close at seven of a Saturday night!"

"Good God!" somebody muttered. Mr. King and Doc Carey started toward me.

"I'll thank you not to be profane!" I said, as I sank onto the folding chair usually reserved for such ancients as Mr. Purdy Brown.

18

✿✿✿✿✿✿✿✿✿✿✿

I am told that I passed out and that Mr. King caught
me just in time to keep me from falling off the folding
chair and hitting the floor. I am thankful for his agility.
I am sorry to say that I can merely report secondhand
what happened during the next thirty-six hours, for although I was unconscious only a little while, something
in my head was definitely out of order. I am told that
Mr. King rode with me in the Rescue Squad ambulance
to the Bent City Hospital, that Trooper Woolridge provided an escort, and that I talked a lot. With the com-
bination of blue and red flashing lights and the sirens,
Arnold's Corners had its biggest night in years. It is
ironic that the one person in Arnold's Corners who
might have enjoyed such a ruckus—namely me—
should not even be able to remember it, due to the con-
cussion. I spent one night in the hospital and came
home under my own steam, but Sunday is a blank in
my personal recollections to this day.

My memory takes up again on Monday morning, although at the time I did not know it was Monday. I woke with a clear head to see Daddy, of all people, sitting by my bed. His face was pale, but he did not look sick anymore. When I opened my eyes he leaned forward and stared at me like he was examining a strange bug under a microscope.

"Hey!" I said. I put a hand up and felt a thick square bandage plastered to my forehead with adhesive tape.

"Hey, yourself. Do you feel all right?"

"Well, of course I feel all right! Why shouldn't I?"

He sat back, his face a mixture of relief, exasperation, and plain worn-outness. "You needn't get on a high horse! You have *not* been right in the head for two nights and a day in between!" He got up and went to the door. "Elizabeth!"

I sat up in bed as Mom's footsteps came light and quick down the hall and into the living room, then into my room.

"Thank the Lord!" she said, after she had looked me in the eye in the same manner as Daddy had done. The two of them stood side by side, gazing down at me as though I were the risen Lazarus or something. I began to feel uneasy. Two nights and a day in between? I counted on my fingers. Saturday night—Sunday—Sunday night. This had to be Monday morning.

"Who's minding the store?" I asked.

Daddy almost smiled. "You'd be surprised."

"Well, who? I hope not Randy Mitchell, after he went off and left the place standing wide open Saturday night. And to think I paid that rascal *double wages* . . ." I looked up at Daddy. "I owe the cash register five dollars. I'll pay it back."

"Now, hold on there," Daddy said, sitting in the chair again. Mom hovered around me, smoothing covers and punching pillows. "Randy didn't go off and leave the place standing open. He closed at seven and brought the key here."

"But why—how did—?"

"You mean why was every man in Arnold's Corners except your daddy in that store Saturday night? They were all getting ready to go search for you, that's what."

I stared. "For *me!* But I didn't need to be searched for! I wasn't lost—"

"How were we to know that?" Daddy retorted. "You created a major crisis in this community! You ought to be paddled, except for the fact that you kept something worse from happening."

"Tal, don't get her all upset," Mom fussed.

"I do not understand," I said. "I hope you will be so kind as to begin at the beginning."

"All right, I will. I was lying on the sofa in the living room when Randy came here at seven fifteen Saturday asking for you. When your mother told him you were at the store closing up, he announced that *he* had been keeping store since five o'clock at your request because *you* had told *him* you needed to be here helping *her*."

Daddy looked at me with some severity. I felt myself blushing.

"We didn't know what to think of that. He gave us the key and the money and left—said he had a date. And here your mom and I didn't have the least idea where you were."

"I thought all kinds of things," Mom put in, "none of them especially good."

"You ought to trust me more than that," I said.

"If you ever give us reason, we certainly will!" Daddy snorted.

I did not argue the point. We come at life from different angles.

"Anyhow," he went on, "we debated what to do. Your mom had just decided that she should go over to Jenny's to see if you were there, when somebody ran up on the porch and pounded on the door." He paused. "Scared us both half out of our wits. It was Lyman Hayes—said he'd found you in the woods back of his house and you'd fallen off your bicycle and hit your head, and that you were on his sofa in need of a doctor."

"I sure was," I sighed, remembering the former pain in my head.

"Your mom could scarcely tolerate the notion that you had been left alone in that condition."

"Well, neither could you!" Mom said.

"So she grabbed up Timmy, got in Lyman's truck, and had him drive her to Jenny's, so Jenny could keep Timmy until you were taken care of."

"Mr. King was there when we drove up," Mom told me. "His camper was parked in front of her house."

"So that's where he was!" I said. "Not even down in the woods at all! I'll be—"

"Mr. Lyman said you had tried to tell him that Mr. King was in danger, but after he saw the camper at Jenny's, he just chuckled and said the kind of danger King was in now was not the kind the law could rescue him from."

Mom and Daddy apparently considered that to be a good joke. I did not get the point.

"Anyhow," Daddy continued, "Jenny took Timmy. King volunteered to go for Doc Carey and bring him to Lyman's. Your mom and Lyman went tearing down the highway to his house, but when they got there, you were gone. Lyman didn't know what to think, as he had told you to stay put, and he hadn't been gone more than twenty-five minutes in all."

I recalled the truck that had turned into Mr. Lyman's driveway. "It seemed longer than that," I said. "It seemed like hours. I thought—"

"Where in the world did you disappear to?" Daddy asked. "They didn't see a sign of you, coming back on the highway. They stopped at Hooker's and he called the highway patrol—"

"How'd he do that—by smoke signal?"

"He's had him a phone installed," Daddy said. "And I am going to do the same after this. Where did you disappear to?"

It seemed silly to tell, in broad daylight. "My brains were mixed up," I excused myself. "I thought Bill Steed's crowd would be looking for me. I stayed in the ditch a lot."

"Why did you think that? You aren't anything to Bill, except a pesky nuisance! He would never seek out your company on purpose."

I had not thought about it in those terms. "May told me—" I began, then stopped. I did not want to get May in trouble again. I thought about the earlier episode and sighed. Knocking my brains loose hadn't been such a bad thing after all. At least it had made me forget, for a little while, how complicated life can be.

"And what did she tell you?" Daddy prompted.

"If you hadn't been sick in bed Saturday night, would you've been somewhere else?" I asked.

"You know that I stay home Saturday nights," he answered.

So I told them what May had seen and heard at the tobacco shed and then Mr. Lewis' remark at the store.

164

"I put two and two together and came up with a hasty conclusion," I said, ashamed to look Daddy in the eye. "I didn't think you would join up with Bill Steed for anything, but—"

Daddy didn't act indignant as I thought he would. "But you weren't sure," he finished for me.

I nodded.

He was thoughtful for a moment. "Lewis did come and talk to me. Said I of all people had a bone to pick with the stranger, and that I needed to show my neighbors whose side I was on."

"And what did you say?" I asked in a small voice.

"I told him," said Daddy, "that as far as I knew, King hadn't done anything to harm a soul in Arnold's Corners, and unless they came up with evidence to the contrary, he could count me out of their little party."

Something heavy lifted from my chest. I leaned over and hugged him tight. He tried not to look too pleased.

"I had thought," he went on, "that they would call it off. Or maybe I was just hoping, because I didn't want to be the one to stick my neck out and tell King what was brewing. Now I wish I had. Some of the men were making ready to go after him when the word came that you were hurt and missing and that everybody was needed to look for you. I guess nobody wanted to look like they were responsible for your disappearance. That's why you saw so many people at the store. Most of them were already charged up for the evening. As I say, what you did was foolish, but it kept something really ugly from happening. Arnold's Corners owes you a debt."

I looked him full in the eye. I had never thought to hear him say such a thing as that, especially now when it seemed so far from the truth.

"What's kept them from jumping Mr. King since Saturday night?" I asked. "Has he left for good?"

Daddy's eyes positively twinkled. "They better not jump him! He's minding the store for me this morning."

I was astounded. Mom and Daddy laughed outright.

"Now, *he* has a story to tell," Daddy said at last, wiping laughter tears from the corners of his eyes. "I will let him tell you—he is planning to come see you this morning. Let your mind be at rest, though—your Mr. King is no longer in trouble in Arnold's Corners."

"You cannot leave me in suspense!" I said, grabbing his sleeve. "I am liable to have a relapse and get brain fever."

Daddy stood up, not in the least perturbed. "I will take a chance on that."

As you have already seen, my daddy cannot be threatened.

Mom obviously felt sorry for me, knowing how hard it is to endure suspense. She put Timmy in the living room in his playpen and fixed a place for me on the sofa. She said I could walk around some but was not to get rambunctious until I had the word from Doc Carey. I assured her that I did not feel in the least rambunctious.

"Do you remember what Trooper Woolridge told you yesterday morning before we left the hospital?" she asked.

My heart bumped. I did not even remember being in the hospital! I shook my head.

"He said the damage claims in the wreck would be settled out of court and that you needn't worry about appearing as a witness."

I was so relieved I could have cried.

"You looked at him sort of wild-eyed and said something about Providence," Mom went on, frowning slightly. "It didn't make sense to me."

"I'm not surprised," I mumbled. "I don't suppose you have conversed with Mrs. Crifton by any chance recently?" I tried to keep my face usual.

Mom looked at me with interest. "Why, yes, as a matter of fact. She brought two lemon pies and said to tell you she could never thank you enough for suggesting that she have Jenny design her dress. She said it was the first time in her life she had been proud of the way she looked, and that she can hardly wait until Doreen's wedding day."

She added, "I pretended to know exactly what she was talking about."

I yelled "*Yippee!*" and spent the next few minutes explaining about J. Chapman, designer, and salesmanship —to Mom's eternal amazement.

"I do not understand how you got to be the way you are!" she said, shaking her head. "I believe your mind stays awake all night while the rest of you is sleeping!"

There might be something to that, but I could not debate the subject with her because just then Mr. King arrived. I was very glad to see him in the flesh, as there had been times on Saturday night that I had not thought to see him in that condition ever again.

"I was worried about you, Lady Rose," he said, taking the seat Mom offered. "After all, it was because of me that you were hurt."

I shook my head. "You are not to feel responsible. You didn't tell me to fall in a hole and hit my head on a rock!"

"If you hadn't, I might not be here now," he replied. He was not joking. It was a chilling thought.

"Do you consider storekeeping a step up or a step

down from wall painting?" I asked, to change the subject. It was a perfectly honest question, but Mr. King laughed so hard I thought I was going to have to be severe with him. Mom joined in, and Timmy, too, although he did not get the joke any more than I did.

"You two need to have a long conversation," said Mom, taking Timmy out of his pen. "Excuse us—we have things to do."

"I'll have to level with you, Lady Rose," Mr. King said, getting serious again. "I'm not sure whether you'll forgive me, especially after all you've been through on my account."

"Try me," I said.

"Well, when I let you—and the other folks in Arnold's Corners—think that I was a wall painter, I wasn't being absolutely truthful."

My heart sank in spite of me. I had thought that here was at least *one* grown-up who could be trusted.

"I do paint walls, sort of," he said. "Sometimes I paint *pictures* on walls."

It did not take long for the light to dawn.

"You mean—? *That's* why you can draw so well! It's not a hobby—you're really and truly an artist, aren't you?" I shouted.

"That's right. I teach in the School of Design at State University."

"It's probably a good thing you didn't tell the whole truth after all," I said, thinking it over. "I am sure some folks around here would have second thoughts about their hard-earned taxes paying a fellow to teach picture-painting instead of doing a good honest day's work."

"That may have been true last week." He chuckled. "But thanks to you everything has changed. As of Saturday night, everybody in Arnold's Corners knows why I am here, and they not only approve, they are also cooperating."

He was enjoying my mystification. "Haven't you wondered what I was doing in Arnold's Corners?" he asked.

I looked down at my hands. "Yes," I admitted, "but you will notice that I have refrained from asking."

"Yes, I noticed. You are a rare person. I should have told you at the beginning. I was commissioned by the state to do a mural for the new Agricultural Research Building on the university campus. The committee decided that since so many people in this state have their roots in the land, nothing would be more appropriate than to have the mural depict 'the essence of rural life.'"

"The essence of rural life?" I repeated. "What's 'essence'?"

"I was afraid you'd ask," he said, scratching his head. "I suppose you could say it is what you have left when you've cleared away all the outside trappings. The part that is permanent—unchangeable."

I made a face. "That is the problem—all the stuff in Arnold's Corners is permanent and unchangeable! That is why May and I are going to leave when we are eighteen."

"For once, I don't agree with you," Mr. King said. "I predict that someday even Arnold's Corners folks will accept one another—and outsiders too—for themselves, and not make judgments by appearances or by how a man makes his living."

"Arnold's Corners has a long way to go in that respect," I sighed.

"No doubt. But at least one person here has an open

mind and that is an excellent beginning, especially since she is young. Of course, she keeps threatening to go away and never come back . . ."

He gave me a meaningful look. "But to continue my story. I must admit I was not too crazy about the idea. In the spring I had just about decided to throw it back at them and tell them to get someone else to paint their 'rural essence'—I wasn't interested. As a matter of fact, I was on my way down to the coast to sulk when I had a flat tire on the highway in Arnold's Corners, in front of Mr. Hayes's house."

"Providence!" I said.

"Very likely," he said solemnly. "It even led Mr. Lyman to come out and give me a hand with the jack."

"Mr. *Lyman?* And you a perfect stranger?"

He nodded. "We hit it off right away. I started getting ideas. By the time I got the spare on, I had asked him if I could come back to stay a few weeks in the summer if I provided my own living quarters. He agreed—you know the rest."

"You mean Mr. Lyman knew all this time that you were an artist?"

"Yes, he knew. But I told him I'd as soon not let the word get around. I thought I'd have a better chance of getting acquainted with people if they didn't know my real reason for being here. I didn't want everyone running to put on his best Sunday clothes every time I came in sight. I wanted sketches of people working, talking, playing. Well, I suppose I was so intent on capturing the everydayness of Arnold's Corners it never crossed my mind I might be getting myself into trouble. Meeting you and Mr. Lyman fooled me into thinking that I'd be accepted by everyone else, no questions asked."

My smile was one-sided. "You didn't know you'd met the only two mavericks in the whole community, did you?"

"No," he said, "not until the damage was done. I kept thinking that things were bound to get better, but when my drawings were stolen, I'll confess I was ready to throw in the towel and shake the dust of Arnold's Corners off my feet."

I had all but forgotten the stolen sketches. "Did you get them back?"

"Yes. Saturday night Mr. Lyman did some explaining to the folks in the store while we were on the way to the hospital. The sketches showed up on his porch the next morning, in good shape."

"Thank goodness!" I breathed. "Do you know who took them?"

He shook his head. "No, and I don't really care. Whoever did it was sorry enough to leave a large watermelon as a peace offering. I'll bring it when I come to dinner tonight."

"Are you coming to dinner here?" I squealed.

"You bet. I'm bringing Jenny and Ruthie too. Your mom and dad wanted to celebrate your recovery—you gave them quite a scare." He leaned forward and spoke in a low voice. "They may never tell you, but to them you are a real heroine."

My throat got lumpy for no reason.

"Got some dust in my eyes," I mumbled, rubbing at them with the back of my hand.

"Sure," he said and handed me his handkerchief.

Dinner at our house that evening was a rousing occasion, even though I had to be dignified due to the condition of my head. Mr. King arrived with the watermelon and Jenny and Ruthie, as promised. Jenny wore a red dress, which she said was the first outfit she had made for herself since she came to Arnold's Corners. It was an exclusive original. She came over and took my hands and kissed me on my bandaged forehead. I do not usually care for that kind of sissy stuff, but this time I did not mind.

"Rosalee," she said, "you are responsible for everything good that has happened to me since I came here."

Well, that was an overwhelming statement from a grown-up. I did not know what to say.

"I can never repay you," she went on. "But when the day comes that you prefer skirts to jeans and shorts, I will design a dress especially for you."

"I appreciate that," I said, "and I am glad you put in that condition, as it may be several years before I am ready."

Everybody laughed.

In the living room after dinner Timmy and Ruthie had a glorious time in the playpen shouting each other down. I sat propped up on sofa pillows and listened to the grown-up conversation about when Mr. King would go back to State University and how Jenny was going to manage her new designing business and whether the Democrats would get back in so Daddy could be postmaster again. I was pleased to be with the four grown-ups I admire most in life, but something was missing. Everyone, including the babies, was in pairs.

Except me.

"What's the matter, Lady Rose?" Mr. King asked quietly. "You are looking very solemn, for such a happy occasion."

"I am having a spell of Double Vision," I told him. "It will pass."

Mom sat forward. "What? Are your eyes hurting? Can't you see clearly? Oh, dear, I was *afraid* you'd get too excited!"

I was sorry I had opened my mouth. Mr. King was the only person who would understand. Luckily a knock sounded at that moment. Daddy went to the door.

"Hey, Mr. Brigham, I'm sorry I couldn't come earlier," said May's voice. "We just got back from Bent City—I brought Rosalee a present."

Well, I had been dignified as long as I could stand it. I let out a holler and threw a pillow in the air, and Daddy showed May in and we hugged each other and the grown-ups laughed and for the remainder of the evening it was just like the lady correspondent for the Bent City *Times* always says—a good time was had by *all!*

Postscript

❀❀❀❀❀❀❀❀❀❀❀

You will be interested to know that every citizen of Arnold's Corners—including May and me—who was sketched by Mr. King has been immortalized in oils on the walls of the Agricultural Research Building. In color. Some might consider it a dubious kind of fame, but Arnold's Corners is enjoying it. Mrs. Crifton is there, larger than life—if that is possible—and looking like a duchess in her sky-blue gown, with the pink and aqua house in the background. Mr. King painted it so the aqua of the house and the blue of the dress do not clash but look extremely distinguished. He is a great artist.

I have heard that when Bill Steed goes to the state capitol, he makes a point of stopping at the university campus to visit the Agricultural Research Building. They say he stands by the portrait of himself so people will see his likeness and recognize him. I do not know if it is true—you know how people make up stuff in Arnold's Corners.

174

Daddy's business has grown so much he is going to have to add onto the store. There are many reasons for it happening, but I am thankful to say that my posing in the post office window in Mrs. Crifton's dress was not one of them. That is a buried-in-the-past secret, I hope. Having Brigham's Store painted on the walls of the Agricultural Research Building has helped, no doubt, as people from all over have come to look at it. But, in addition, Daddy now takes credit cards. And he has given over the front post office corner to Peter York Hopper and R. D.'s Effervescent Mouthwash display. The Federal Government eased him and Mr. Hooker out of their rivalry by deciding to build a new brick post office. Mavis Edwards is the new postmistress. She tells me every time Jenny gets a letter from Mr. King— as if it was any of my business! People are always asking me when they will get married. I do not know. I would not tell if I did. But I will say that Jenny does not need to get married if she does not want to because she is designing exclusive originals not only for ladies in Arnold's Corners but also for some in Bent City and beyond. She now displays her outfits in the window of the Exclusive Shoppe in Bent City, where Mom used to work. They look better on the dummies than they ever would on me. It is how they are pinned, I guess.

May and I have earned a considerable amount in our baby-sitting business, Jenny being so busy now that she has to have both of us. Since school began, we have been taking turns in the afternoons. May has also come in on the book-trading arrangement with Jenny and me. Among us we can get thirty books—one a day, like vitamins. I am the only one who reads all thirty, though.

May and I are each putting aside a little bit of our

earnings every week for when we are old enough to leave Arnold's Corners. However, I will have to admit that my attitude toward the place has changed somewhat. I still do not wish to be a narrow person, but on the other hand, Arnold's Corners *does* have some characteristics that are worthy of note, not the least being that when you are hurt and lost, the people here will go look for you. I expect I will remember some of them with affection after I have left to go on my world travels. I will, no doubt, come back from time to time. And if, in my judgment, it appears that Mr. King's prediction is coming true, then perhaps when all my money is spent and my travels are over, I will come back to stay in Arnold's Corners.